ENGLISH THROUGH IDIOMS

by Anita Wu
Mark A. Pengra

LEARNING PUBLISHING
CO., LTD.

　　學英文的人，常常會有一種感觸，或許您也碰到過這類問題，那就是放在您眼前的每個英文單字您都懂，可是當它們合力「團結」起來的時候，您就是硬被它們打敗了。真是奇妙！這是什麼玩意？——答案是**片語**。

✄ 從趣味中，主宰生活必備片語！✄

　　英文片語是活用英語的泉源，簡簡單單的幾個字，運用得巧妙的話，就可以讓您在英語世界打遍天下無敵手。孫子兵法上說：「知己知彼，百戰不殆。」本書的意旨，就是在「趣味性」的原則下，使您迅速、有效地記憶與學習。我們精選一連串與生活密切相關的片語，採分類密集編排的科學方法，編寫成「**英文片語趣味記憶法**」，激發您驚人的潛能，使您在短短的一個月內，就可成為英語的行家！

✄ 片語趣味記憶法，每天用得上！✄

● **天天動腦記憶法**：取材各種場合的生活實況及必備會話用語，讓您在任何場所，實際派上用場。

● **分秒必爭記憶法**：採分類系統之整理，節省記憶的時間，熟悉各種時間狀況的說法及數量單位的運用。

- **熱門動詞記憶法**：從掌握十二個基本動詞開始，倍增您英文
  片語的實力，並按字母之順序編排最常用的生活語，解
  釋詳盡，易學易記。

- **介詞情侶記憶法**：精選四組相對的慣用介系詞，對照學習，
  簡潔的編排，記得快，背得容易。

- **肢體聯想記憶法**：配合趣味的圖畫，把握肢體的特性，使您
  輕鬆地學好各種肢體訊息。

　　本書的另一特色就是版面清新活潑，讓您看得舒適，可以
輕鬆地記憶。為求完美，成書的每一階段皆十分謹慎，然付梓在
即，恐仍有疏忽之處，尚祈各界先進不吝批評指教。

　　　　　　　　　　　　　　　　　編者　謹識

CONTENTS

Part 4 熱門動詞記憶法 **69**

Part 5 介詞情侶記憶法 **141**

Part 6 肢體聯想記憶法 **183**

使用說明

　　單字和片語是相輔相成的。背好英文單字的下一步，就是**活用英文片語**；而將英文片語記熟之後，駕馭單字及句子的功力自不在話下。

　　但英文片語支解開來，字字簡單，組合排列，却讓人容易混淆，不知如何用起。本書特針對**一般社會人士**及**在學學生**此種需要，深入片語心臟，詳細分割成五大類，並附實用例句、自我測量，迅速驗收您的學習成效。

- **分類**：全書採特殊分類記憶法，由**生活**、**時間**、**動詞**、**介詞**及**肢體**等五方面著手，務使您在最短的時間內，發揮最大效率。

- **例句**：豐富實用的例句，緊附在每個片語之後，讓您**對照學習**，加深印象。

- **圖解**：以可愛生動的插圖，讓您在閱讀或背誦的時候，加點**想像及喘息**的時空。

- **註釋**：註解詳盡，將針對讀者速讀與精讀雙管齊下的需求，節省您**查字典**的時間。

- **自我測量**：掌握語言學習新趨勢，設計自我練習，讓讀者測試一下自己的英文程度之定位，才能**調適方向**，積極訓練。

Editorial Staff

● 企劃・編著 / 武藍蕙
● 英文撰稿
　Mark A. Pengra ・ Bruce S. Stewart
　Edward C. Yulo ・ John C. Didier
● 校訂
　劉　毅・葉淑霞・黃欽成・王慶銘・王怡華
　曾蕙蘭・陳怡平・林　婷・陳威如・陳斯如
● 校閱
　Larry J. Marx ・ Lois M. Findler
　John H. Voelker ・ Keith Gaunt
● 封面設計 / 張鳳儀
● 插畫 / 蘇翠鳳
● 版面設計 / 張鳳儀
● 版面構成 / 黃春蓮・林麗鳳・蘇翠鳳・謝淑敏
● 打字
　黃淑貞・吳秋香・倪秀梅・蘇淑玲
　洪桂美・徐湘君
● 校對
　黃惠美・林韶慧・卓永堅・林順隆
　邱蔚獎・陳騏永・宋美明・朱輝錦

PART 1

親近英文片語
腦力激盪的第一步

您認得下列這些片語嗎？

A

☐☐ a cup of　　　　　　　　　形　1 杯的

☐☐ a few　　　　　　　　　　形　少數的；數（個）

☐☐ after school　　　　　　　副　放學後

☐☐ a kind〔sort〕of　　　　形　一種的

☐☐ a little　　　　　　　　　形　少量的；一些

☐☐ all day〔night〕（ long ）　副　整天（晚）（之久）

☐☐ all right　　　　　　　　形副　好；無恙

☐☐ a lot of　　　　　　　　　形　很多的

☐☐ apart from　　　　　　　　介　除了～之外

☐☐ a piece of　　　　　　　　形　一片的

☐☐ arrive at〔in〕　　　　　動　到達

☐☐ as ～ as possible　　　　副　儘可能～

☐☐ as soon as　　　　　　　　連　即刻

☐☐ at home　　　　　　　　　副　在家

☐☐ at last　　　　　　　　　副　最後

☐☐ at once　　　　　　　　　副　立刻

☐☐ at school　　　　　　　　形副　在學校；上課中

☐☐ at（the）table　　　　　副　用餐中

☐☐ away from　　　　　　　　介　從～離開

B

☐☐ be careful of　　　　　　動　小心；注意

♋ 參考左頁，把適當的字填入空格裏。(答案見 p.16)

1. 蘇珊用了很多糖。

   Susan used **a** _____ **of** sugar.

2. 他一上床，立刻就睡著了。

   He fell asleep **as** _____ **as** he went to bed.

3. 你應該馬上走。

   You should go **at** _____ .

4. 讓我們喝杯茶吧。

   Let's have **a** _____ **of** tea.

5. 請給我一片蛋糕。

   Please give me **a** _____ **of** cake.

6. 紐約離東京很遠。

   New York is far **away** _____ Tokyo.

7. 他有一些朋友。

   He has **a** _____ friends.

8. 他們有些希望。

   They had **a** _____ hope.

9. 他儘可能跑得快。

   He ran **as fast as** _____ .

10. 除了價錢之外，這帽子不適合我。

    Apart _____ the cost, the hat doesn't suit me.

11. 他終於成功了。

    At _____ he succeeded.

12. 煤炭是石頭的一種。

    Coal is **a** _____ **of** stone.

您認得下列這些片語嗎？

☐☐ be close to	動	接近
☐☐ be famous for	動	以～出名
☐☐ be filled with	動	充滿
☐☐ be full of	動	裝滿
☐☐ be glad to do	動	高興做～
☐☐ be going to do	動	將要～
☐☐ be late for	動	遲到
☐☐ be pleased to do	動	高興做～
☐☐ both A and B		A、B兩者
☐☐ bring A to B	動	持A至B
☐☐ bring about	動	使發生；致使
☐☐ build up	動	增加；加強
☐☐ burn down	動	燒毀
☐☐ by airplane	副	搭飛機
☐☐ by mail〔airmail〕	副	郵寄（航空信）
☐☐ by (tele)phone	副	打電話
☐☐ by the way	副	再者；此外

C

☐☐ call at	動	訪問（家、地）
☐☐ call on	動	拜訪（人）
☐☐ clear up	動	放晴
☐☐ come (a)round	動	來臨
☐☐ come back	動	回來

☺ 參考左頁，把適當的字填入空格裏。（答案見 p. 16 ）

1. 聖誕節很快就要來了。

   Christmas will **come** _____ very soon.

2. 請你用航空郵寄的方式寄這封信好嗎？

   Would you send this letter **by** _____ ?

3. 我明天能去拜訪她。

   I can **call** _____ her tomorrow.

4. 我們的學校很靠近車站。

   Our school **is** very **close** _____ the station.

5. 瑪麗今天上學遲到。

   Mary **was late** _____ school today.

6. 賭博導致他的毀滅。

   Gambling _____ **about** his ruin.

7. 他會在六點以後回來。

   He will **come** _____ after six.

8. 她的房間充滿了洋娃娃。

   Her room **was filled** _____ dolls.

9. 她很欣喜地接受他的求婚。

   She **was** _____ **to** accept his proposal.

10. 那棟建築昨夜被燒毀。

    That building **burned** _____ last night.

11. 這個地方以風景優美而聞名。

    The place **is famous** _____ its scenic beauty.

** proposal〔prə'pozḷ〕*n*. 求婚　　scenic〔'sinɪk〕*adj*. 風景的

您認得下列這些片語嗎？

☐☐	come by	動 走近；經過
☐☐	come down	動 下來；降下
☐☐	come in	動 進入
☐☐	come into	動 進入（場所、狀態）
☐☐	come out	動 出現
☐☐	come over	動 訪問；發生
☐☐	come to	動 總數達～
☐☐	come up（to）	動 前來

▌D

☐☐	depend on〔upon〕	動 依賴

▌F

☐☐	far from	介 離～很遠
☐☐	for long	副 很久（＝ *for a long time*）
☐☐	from door to door	副 挨家挨戶
☐☐	from morning till〔to〕night	副 從早到晚
☐☐	from the beginning	副 最初；開始

▌G

☐☐	get at〔in〕	動 到達
☐☐	get on	動 登上
☐☐	get to	動 開始；著手

☺ 參考左頁，把適當的字填入空格裏。(答案見 p.16)

1. 他是個可依賴的男人。

   He is a man to be **depended** _____ .

2. 當公車來時，她就上車。

   When the bus came, she **got** _____ .

3. 他進入我的私室。

   He **came** _____ my private room.

4. 這家人不會離開很久。

   The family won't be away **for** _____ .

5. 他們從早到晚工作。

   They worked **from morning** _____ **night**.

6. 明天下午我會經過這兒。

   I'll **come** _____ tomorrow afternoon.

7. 總額達十元。

   The sum **came** _____ ten dollars.

8. 我的家鄉離東京不遠。

   My home town isn't **far** _____ Tokyo.

9. 「進來，」布朗太太說。

   " **Come** _____ ," said Mrs. Brown.

10. 他從倫敦來看我。

    He **came** _____ from London to see me.

11. 湯姆起身下樓到廚房來。

    Tom got up and **came** _____ to the kitchen.

12. 我搆不到天花板。

    I can't **get** _____ the ceiling.

您認得下列這些片語嗎？

☐☐	get up	動	起床；起來
☐☐	get well	動	恢復
☐☐	go after	動	追求
☐☐	go away	動	離去
☐☐	go back	動	回去
☐☐	go by	動	過去；逝去
☐☐	go down	動	下；落
☐☐	go for	動	去獲得（買、找）
☐☐	go for a walk	動	散步
☐☐	go in	動	進入
☐☐	go into	動	進入（房間等）
☐☐	good luck	名	幸運
☐☐	go out	動	出去
☐☐	go (a)round	動	四處走動
☐☐	go through	動	穿過；通過
☐☐	go to bed	動	上床睡覺
☐☐	go up	動	（物價）上昇；高漲
☐☐	grow up	動	長大；成人

H

☐☐	had better		毋寧；較為適宜或聰明地
☐☐	have school	動	在上學
☐☐	hear from	動	得到消息；接到信
☐☐	hear of	動	聽說（消息）

☺ 參考左頁，把適當的字填入空格裏。(答案見 p.16)

1. 她下週將離去。

   She is **going** _____ next week.

2. 年歲逝去。

   Years **went** _____ .

3. 你最好趕快。

   You **had** _____ hurry.

4. 石油的價格又上漲了。

   The price of petroleum has **gone** _____ again.

5. 他拿了帽子，然後出去。

   He took his hat and **went** _____ .

6. 每個月我都接到朋友的信。

   I **hear** _____ my friend every month.

7. 他打開門進去。

   He opened the door and **went** _____ .

8. 不要追求名聲。

   Don't **go** _____ fame.

9. 他下樓梯。

   He **went** _____ the stairs.

10. 幸好雨停了。

    By **good** _____ , it stopped raining.

11. 聽到他突然死亡，我很震驚。

    I'm shocked to **hear** _____ his sudden death.

** petroleum〔pəˈtrolɪəm〕*n*. 石油

您認得下列這些片語嗎？

I

☐ in bed　　　　　　　　　副 臥；睡
☐ in front of　　　　　　　介 在～前面
　　反 at the back of　　　反 在～後面
☐ in order to (do)　　　　副 爲了～
☐ in time　　　　　　　　副 及時

K

☐ knock at〔on〕　　　　　動 敲擊

L

☐ later on　　　　　　　　副 稍後
☐ laugh at　　　　　　　　動 嘲笑
☐ lead A to B　　　　　　動 引導A至B
☐ listen to　　　　　　　　動 傾聽
☐ little by little　　　　　副 漸漸地；漸次地
☐ look for　　　　　　　　動 尋找
☐ lots of　　　　　　　　　形 許多的

N

☐ near by　　　　　　　　副 形 在附近
☐ near to　　　　　　　　介 接近
☐ next to　　　　　　　　介 隔鄰

☺ 參考左頁，把適當的字填入空格裏。(答案見 p.17)

1. 他不會聽我的忠告。
   He would not **listen**＿＿＿＿＿ my advice.

2. 房子前面有棵樹。
   A tree stood in＿＿＿＿＿ **of** the house.

3. 他坐在我隔壁。
   He sat **next** ＿＿＿＿＿ me.

4. 我敲門。
   I **knocked** ＿＿＿＿＿ the door.

5. 她有很多朋友。
   He has **lots** ＿＿＿＿＿ friends.

6. 他們嘲笑那個遇到麻煩的人。
   They **laughed** ＿＿＿＿＿ the man in trouble.

7. 他出國是爲了研讀法律。
   He went abroad in＿＿＿＿＿ **to** study law.

8. 我家接近車站。
   My house is **near**＿＿＿＿＿ the station.

9. 這家人正在找一幢出租的房子。
   The family is **looking** ＿＿＿＿＿ a house for rent.

10. 湯姆還在睡。
    Tom is still **in**＿＿＿＿＿.

11. 他及時趕到吃晚餐。
    He arrived in＿＿＿＿＿ for dinner.

12. 我稍候會向你解釋情況。
    I will explain the situation to you **later**＿＿＿＿＿.

您認得下列這些片語嗎？

□□ not ~ any more　　　　　不再～
　　〔longer〕

□□ not only A but　　　　　不只A而且B
　　（also）B

▌O

□□ of course　　　　　　　副 當然
□□ on one's〔the〕way　　　副 在某人的途中
□□ over there〔here〕　　　副 在那裏（這裏）

▌P

□□ pass by　　　　　　　　動 經過；時間消失
□□ play the piano　　　　　動 彈鋼琴
□□ plenty of　　　　　　　形 充分的
□□ put down　　　　　　　動 放下
□□ put in　　　　　　　　動 進入
□□ put up　　　　　　　　動 供膳宿

▌R

□□ ring up　　　　　　　動 打電話
□□ run away　　　　　　　動 跑開
□□ run down　　　　　　　動 跑下
□□ run into　　　　　　　動 跑入
□□ run off　　　　　　　動 逃跑

☺ 參考左頁，把適當的字填入空格裏。(答案見 p. 17)

1. 他們今天在一家小旅舍投宿。

   They **put** _____ at an inn today.

2. 你看有個紳士在那兒。

   You see a gentleman_____ **there.**

3. 當然是真的！

   _____**course** it's true !

4. 狗兒儘快地逃跑開。

   The dog **ran** _____ as fast as it could.

5. 小偷跑走了。

   The thief **ran** _____.

6. 我們需要充分的空間。

   We need _____ **of** space.

7. 他跑入房間。

   He **ran** _____ the room.

8. 我們再也受不了這股熱氣。

   We can't stand the heat _____ **more.**

9. 我在上學的途中遇見他。

   I met him_____ **my way** to school.

10. 明天打電話給我。

    Ring me_____tomorrow.

11. 他將眼鏡放在桌上。

    He **put** his glasses_____ on the desk.

12. 一年一年很快過去。

    The years quickly **pass**_____.

您認得下列這些片語嗎？

S

☐☐ set up   動 設立

☐☐ slow down   動 將速度減慢

☐☐ so ～ that ～   連 如此～以致於～

☐☐ speak to   動 和人說話

☐☐ stand by   動 旁觀；援助

☐☐ such ～ that ～   這樣～以致於～

T

☐☐ take A to B   動 帶A至B

☐☐ take a walk   動 散步

☐☐ take care of   動 照顧

☐☐ take in   動 接受；容納

☐☐ take off   動 （飛機）起飛；離陸

☐☐ talk over   動 談論

☐☐ talk to   動 訓戒；斥責

☐☐ talk with   動 和～談話

☐☐ these days   副 最近

W

☐☐ wake up   動 醒來

☐☐ write to   動 寫信給～

☺ 參考左頁，把適當的字填入空格裏。(答案見 p.17)

1. 關於那件事，我訓了孩子一頓。

   I **talked** _____ the child about it.

2. 請照料我的小妹妹。

   Please **take care** _____ my little sister.

3. 我們的飛機在下午四點起飛。

   Our plane **takes** _____ at 4 p.m.

4. 他將火車的速度慢下來。

   He **slowed** _____ the train.

5. 他樂意幫助你。

   He's willing to **stand** _____ you.

6. 她每月寫信給母親。

   She **writes** _____ her mother every month.

7. 最近許多老人都單獨生活。

   Many aged people live alone _____ **days**.

8. 我會帶他到銀行。

   I will _____ him **to** the bank.

9. 他們將設立一所新學校。

   They will **set** _____ a new school.

10. 他和她談了很久。

    He **talked** _____ her for a long time.

11. 海綿很快吸收水份。

    Sponges readily **take** _____ water.

** sponge 〔 spʌndʒ 〕 *n.* 海綿

解 答

以下的英文片語，都是最基本而又常用的，您可以依頁數對照看看，前面您做的自我測量答對了幾題？答錯了幾題？哪些片語是您仍須加強的？然後，您就可以翻開下頁，繼續閱讀了。

（ p.3 ）
1. lot
2. soon
3. once
4. cup
5. piece
6. from
7. few
8. little
9. possible
10. from
11. last
12. kind

（ p.5 ）
1. (a)round
2. airmail
3. on

4. to
5. for
6. brought
7. back
8. with
9. pleased
10. down
11. for

（ p.7 ）
1. on
2. on
3. into
4. long
5. till
6. by
7. to
8. from

9. in
10. over
11. down
12. at

（ p.9 ）
1. away
2. by
3. better
4. up
5. out
6. from
7. in
8. after
9. down
10. luck
11. of

（ **p.11** ）

1. to
2. front
3. to
4. at
5. of
6. at
7. order
8. to
9. for
10. bed
11. time
12. on

（ **p.13** ）

1. up
2. over
3. Of
4. off
5. away
6. plenty
7. into
8. any
9. on
10. up
11. down
12. by

（ **p.15** ）

1. to
2. of
3. off
4. down
5. by
6. to
7. these
8. take
9. up
10. with
11. in

● 容易誤譯的慣用語 ●

　　以下為您介紹在翻譯時，容易被誤譯的片語，請先逐次譯出（口譯或筆譯皆可）以下句子，再對照答案，將錯誤的地方多讀幾次，以便牢記。

1. When he heard the news, he *hit the ceiling*.
2. His friends ran away and left him *holding the bag*.
3. She is *in deep water*. I'll help her out.
4. When young, he *sowed his wild oats*.
5. Mother *brings home the bacon*.
6. Don't *burn the candle at both ends*.
7. He *cooked his goose* when he *called* his boss *names*.
8. My naughty brother is *in Dutch* again.
9. Mr. Smith started his business *on a shoe string*.
10. He tried to *pull the wool over* his wife's *eyes*.

《解答》

1. 非常生氣
2. 挑起責任
3. 陷於困境
4. 任性放蕩
5. 養全家

6. 過分消耗精力
7. 毀了機會 / 講壞話
8. 惹麻煩
9. 以一點點的錢
10. 矇騙

PART 2

天天動腦記憶法

來自生活點滴，隨時用得上！

● **天天動腦記憶法的內容** —— 涵蓋食、衣、住、行等生活各個層面的必備片語，您只要動動腦筋，就能馬上開口。

特色 —— 重要生活慣用語分門別類地系統整理，並附精彩佳句、趣味插圖，對照學習，一看就會！

目的 —— 讓您利用平日幾分鐘的時間，熟悉各類已學過或容易忘的慣用語，不知不覺中牢記並活用它們。

要訣 —— 一次只記一大類，慢慢擴大範圍，並儘量在寫作、談話中應用，成為生活中開口說英語的靈魂。

實況生活 ❶ —— 吃飯請客沒煩惱

食（food）、衣（clothes）、住（house）、行（transport）是現代人日常生活中天天接觸得到的事情。在食的方面，本單元特精選一連串簡易實用的英文片語句子，使您一分鐘內學會吃飯請客的遣詞用法，隨時派上用場。

◈ 上館子

☐☐ Let me **treat you** to a Cantonese restaurant.
　　（讓我請你到一家粵菜館吃飯。）

☐☐ I'd like to **sit down** over there near the window.
　　（我想坐在靠窗戶那邊。）

☐☐ May I **look over** the menu？
　　（我可以看看菜單嗎？）

☐☐ **Take your time** deciding. I'll be back in a few minutes.
　　（慢慢決定，過幾分鐘我會再來。）

☐☐ May I **take** your **order** now？
　　（現在您要點些什麼菜呢？）

☐☐ I don't want to eat too much for I am **on a diet**.
　　（我不想吃太多，我正在節食。）

☐☐ **How do you like** your beef steak？
　　（你的牛排要幾分熟？）

實況生活 ❶ ── 吃飯請客沒煩惱

☐☐ It tastes **just right**.

（味道嚐起來剛剛好。）

☐☐ I'd like to have **a cup of** coffee.

（我要一杯咖啡。）

☐☐ May I ask you when's your **day off**?

（請問一下你們的店哪天不營業呢？）

◆ 付帳

☐☐ **Put it on one bill**, please.

（帳請一起算。）

☐☐ Let's **go Dutch**.

（讓我們各付各的。）

☐☐ I'll **pay the bill**.

（我來付錢。）

☐☐ **There's nothing the matter** with this dish.

（這盤菜餚沒有什麼問題。）

☐☐ Please **help yourself**.

（請自行取用。）

☐☐ I **take** milk **with** my coffee.

（我的咖啡要加牛奶。）

☐☐ Please **bring** me the **check**.

（買單。）

◈ 應用會話

C：May I take your order, please?

　　請問要點些什麼呢?

A：Well, I'd like to have orange juice, bacon and eggs, and buttered toast.　What will you have, Jane?

　　嗯,我要柳橙汁,火腿蛋和奶油土司。珍,妳呢?

B：Well, let me see......　I'll just have a cup of coffee.　I don't feel like eating this morning.

　　嗯,讓我想想……我只要一杯咖啡。今天早上我不想吃東西。

A：You'd better eat some breakfast.　It's going to be a long day.

　　妳最好吃點早餐。今天將是漫長的一天。

C：How about a waffle, Miss?　We make delicious waffles.

　　小姐,來點雞蛋餅好嗎?我們做得十分美味可口。

B：All right.　I'll have one.

　　好的,給我來一份。

C：(*To man*) Let's see.　You want orange juice, bacon and eggs, and buttered toast.　(*To woman*) And a waffle and coffee.　Right?

　　(對男人說)我們來看看,你要柳橙汁、火腿蛋和奶油土司。

　　(對女人說)和一份雞蛋餅跟咖啡,對嗎?

A：I'll have coffee, too.

　　我也要咖啡。

No, Thank you

Aunt : Won't you have something more, Jim?

Jim : No, thank you, I'm full.

Aunt : Well, then, put some fruit and cakes in your
pockets. You can eat them *at home*.

Jim : No, thank you. They are full, too.

不了，謝謝你

姨　媽：你不再多吃一點嗎，吉姆？

吉　姆：不了，謝謝，我吃飽了。

姨　媽：噢，那麼你放些水果和蛋糕在口袋裏吧！你可以**在
家**吃。

吉　姆：不了，謝謝。它們也吃飽了。

實況生活 ❷ ── 討價還價有一套

買東西（shopping）本身就是一種藝術，不是吃虧，就是佔便宜，其中蘊含的學問可真不小，各種心理戰術也紛紛出籠，在爾虞我詐之下，如何能創造出自己討價還價（bargaining）的本領，就要靠您自己多去汲取一些實戰的經驗囉！

◈ 購物

☐☐ I'd like to **take a look at** this pair of shoes.
（我想看看這雙鞋子。）

☐☐ I want to **try** this **on**.
（我想試穿看看。）

☐☐ Do you **give discounts**？
（你們有打折嗎？）

☐☐ Don't you **have a second price**？
（不能再便宜一點嗎？）

☐☐ I guess I'll have to **think it over**.
（我想我要考慮一下。）

☐☐ I think I'll **look around** a little more.
（我想四處再逛逛看。）

☐☐ I'll **come back** later.（我待會兒會再來。）

實況生活 ❷ —— 討價還價有一套

◆ 成交

☐☐ I've **made up my mind** to buy the expensive one.
（我決定買貴一點的那個。）

☐☐ I **changed my mind** after I **tried** it **out**.
（在我試驗後，我改變了主意。）

☐☐ I'll **take it**.
（我買了。）

☐☐ Could you **take off** the price tag for me？
（你能幫我撕掉價格標籤嗎？）

☐☐ Please **wrap it up**.
（請包起來。）

☐☐ It is **worth it**！
（划得來！）

☐☐ That's **a good bargain**.
（很划算的買賣。）

☐☐ It is helpful to have my wife **along with** me.
（讓太太陪我去很有幫助。）

◆ 應用會話

B： Good morning, sir. What can I do for you?
　　早安，先生，我能為您效勞嗎？

A： Show me a pair of shoes will you?
　　請拿一雙鞋子給我看看。

B： Yes, sir. This way, please.
　　好的，先生，請這邊走。

A： All right. 好。

B： What size do you wear? 你穿幾號的鞋子？

A： Size 10. 十號。

B： Any particular color? 要什麼特別的顏色嗎？

A： I like black. 我喜歡黑色。

B： How about this pair? 這雙怎麼樣？

A： I don't think so. 不怎麼樣。

B： How about these? 這些呢？

A： I like this pair. Let me try them on.
　　我喜歡這雙，讓我試穿看看。

B： Certainly. Well, they fit you perfectly.
　　當然。嗯，它們很適合你。

A： I'll take them. 我買了。

"up and down" 是說在原地上下移動。譬如 "It goes up and down." 通常用在電梯或蹺蹺板上。至於 ups and downs 則指所謂的榮枯盛衰。感慨人生的浮沈,可說:"The life has its ups and downs."

up and down

國語用「被債壓得轉不動頭」來表示債台高築。而英語則用「債淹到頭」來表現。不管哪一種說法,都出現「頭」這個字,實有異曲同工之妙。

He is up to his neck in debt.

最近很流行 up-to-date 的資訊或 up-to-date 的商店這類話,到底是什麼意思呢?
以 "Make it up-to-date!" 來講,就是 "使合乎潮流" 的意思。(這句話原是簿記用語。)至於 "Update it!",也常在新聞上看到,意思是 "使其更新"。

"Update it!"

實況生活 ❸ ——住得舒服最要緊

出國旅遊（travel abroad）最困擾的，莫過於住的問題。如何開口說要登記住宿（check in）或詢問一些資訊呢？本單元特挑出幾句必備的住宿時的用語供您參考，讓您在面對一些老外服務員，輕鬆自在地表達您所需要的東西。

◆ 住宿辦理

☐☐ We **checked in** at the Hilton Hotel as soon as we arrived.
（我們一到達就到希爾頓飯店辦理住宿登記。）

☐☐ When should we **make a reservation**？
（我們何時該預訂旅館房間呢？）

☐☐ Could you **send someone up** to make the bed？
（請派人來整理牀舖好嗎？）

☐☐ Could you send someone up to **pick up** some laundry？
（請派人來收取送洗的衣服好嗎？）

☐☐ Where can I **get** my money **exchanged**？
（在哪裏可以兌換錢幣？）

☐☐ I'd like to **extend my stay** through Sunday.
（我想延長停留時間到星期天以後再走。）

實況生活 ❸ ── 住得舒服最要緊

☐☐ When should we **check out**?

（我們何時結帳離開旅館呢？）

☐☐ Please **forward my mail** to this address.

（請幫我把郵件轉寄到這個地址。）

❖ 休憩與詢問

☐☐ I am **tired out**, I'll lie down for a while.

（我累死了，要躺一下。）

☐☐ I want to **take a shower** before dinner.

（晚餐前我要沖個澡。）

☐☐ We are **fully booked**.

（我們已經客滿了。）

☐☐ The parking lot is **in the rear of** the hotel.

（停車場在飯店的後面。）

☐☐ Would you **fill** this card **out**?

（請填寫這張卡好嗎？）

☐☐ I'd like a room **with a nice view**.

（我要一間視野良好的房間。）

☐☐ You may **check with** our manager.

（你可以向我們經理詢問。）

◆ 應用會話

A： Have you ever traveled by plane?
　　你曾經搭過飛機旅行嗎?

B： Yes, I went to Hong Kong by air last fall.
　　是的，去年秋天我搭機去香港。

A： How long did it take from Taipei to Hongkong?
　　從台北到香港要花多久時間?

B： Only an hour. 只要一小時。

A： Didn't you get airsick? 你不會暈機嗎?

B： No, I didn't. 是的，我不會暈機。

A： Weren't you scared so high in the air?
　　在那麼高的空中你不會感到害怕嗎?

B： Yes, I was, when the plane hit an air-pocket. But the
　　stewardess told us it was nothing serious, and I calmed
　　down. 會呀，當飛機起飛的時候，我會害怕。但空中小姐告訴我
　　們那沒什麼，我就平靜下來了。

A： Did you get a good view of northern Taiwan?
　　你有沒有欣賞到台灣北部的美好風光呢?

B： I certainly did. The sky was very clear, and we could
　　see for miles and miles.
　　當然有，天空十分晴朗，我們可以一覽無遺。

A： What a lucky fellow you were! 你這傢伙真幸運!

最近，英文報紙的標題上也有
layoff 這個字，解釋為「暫時解
僱」。講求實力的美國社會中，
這是常有的事。

layoff

bricklayer 為磚匠。另外，**layer**
有重疊的意思，所以，**layer cake**
指的是堆了好幾層巧克力或奶油
的海綿蛋糕。以前在日本曾經流
行的 **layered-look**（在長袖襯衫
外，再穿上短袖襯衫的型式），
也是由 **layer** 這個字衍生而來的。

inlay

inlay 是牙齒的鑲補物，常在牙
醫診所裡聽到。

layover 中途下車。

layout 這個字，相信你已經相
當熟悉。除了指房間的佈置，版
面的設計外，也有計劃、一套的
意思。

提到 **layman**, 不知道各位會想到
什麼？在外國，指的是非宗教家
的普通信徒，但也具有「非專家
的普通人」之意。

layout

實況生活 ❹ —— 坐車遇到問題怎樣好

俗語説：「出外條條難。」尤其是到些人生地不熟的地方，格外地需要他人的幫助，可是語言不太通怎麼辦？而英文的單字又嫌太多或太長，記不住，那麼建議您多學些簡單的片語（ short phrases ），旣經濟又實惠。

◆ 坐車

☐☐ Where can I **take the bus**？
　　（我可以在哪裏搭公車呢？）

☐☐ I **missed the bus**. （我沒搭上公車。）

☐☐ I **wait for** the bus to **pick me up**.
　　（我等公車來載我。）

◆ 解決行的問題

☐☐ Say, Conductor! What's **the next stop**?
　　（車掌先生！下一站是什麼？）

☐☐ Would you please tell me when to **get off**?
　　（請告訴我何時下車好嗎？）

☐☐ The train **takes** a lot **longer** to get to Taipei.
　　（火車到台北的時間較長。）

實況生活 ❹ ── 坐車遇到問題怎樣好

□□ How far is it **from** Taipei **to** Kaohsiung？
（從台北到高雄有多遠？）

□□ How long does it take to **get to** the airport？
（到機場要花多久時間？）

□□ Can you tell me **how to get to** the station？
（請告訴我如何到車站？）

◆ 交通狀況

□□ The taxi driver **runs a red light.**
（計程車司機闖紅燈。）

□□ The car has **run out of gas.**
（汽車油料耗盡了。）

□□ We stopped at a **filling station.**
（我們在一個加油站停車。）

□□ The bus **drew up** and we **got on.**
（公車停下來，我們上車。）

□□ **Watch your step!**（小心走路！）

□□ **Go straight on.**（直走。）

□□ **Turn to the left (right).**
（向左〔右〕轉。）

□□ The train was **about to** leave when we arrived.
（當我們抵達時，火車正要開走。）

◈ 應用會話

A : Does this bus go downtown?

這是往市區的公車嗎?

B : No, ma'am, but it meets the No. 67 bus on "B" Avenue. No. 67 passes by the civic center downtown.

不是,女士。不過它會在B街和67號會合。67號公車經過市中心。

A : Then, can I transfer?

那麼,我可以轉車嗎?

B : Yes you can. 可以呀。

A : Thank you. And how long will it take to get downtown?

謝謝。到市區要花多久時間呢?

B : About half an hour. 大約半小時。

A : Please tell me when we get to "B" Avenue, will you?

到B街的時候,請告訴我一聲好嗎?

B : All right. 好的。

I make it 有「成功」的意思,譬如,考試成績不錯,或者是達成什麼目的都可以說。另外,"**I just made it!**",則是「剛好趕上」的意思。

"I just made it!"

提到 **make-up**, 不知會想到什麼?大概是化粧吧。粧化得很濃爲 **heavy make-up**。

那麼 **a makeup exam** 又是什麼呢?就是補考的意思。希望讀者不會常用到:"**Will you let me take a makeup exam?**"

動詞的 **make up**, 則有「賠償」的意思。"**Will you make it up for me?**"(你要賠償我嗎?)

heavy make-up

另外 **make up** 在戀人之間,有重修舊好的意思。例如:"**Let's kiss and make up!**"

關於 **make** 的說明, **do you make sense**?

"Let's kiss and make up!"

實況生活 ❺ ── 談生意用電話洽商

您有沒有過打電話（call，phone）給老外的經驗呢？很緊張、也很刺激，特別是第一次，會有讓您手心冒汗，不知所措的現象，不過講完了，自己也不知道是怎麼活過來的，或許事後回想起來會覺得這種遊戲還蠻好玩的！

◆ 電話聯繫

☐☐ May I **speak to** Mr. Huang？
（我可以跟黃先生講話嗎？）

☐☐ **Hold the line**, please.（請不要掛斷。）

☐☐ I'll **put** you **through**.（我幫你接通。）

☐☐ The **line is busy**.（電話中。）

☐☐ He **stepped out** for a moment.
（他出去一會兒。）

☐☐ Shall I **call back** later？
（我待會兒回電話給你好嗎？）

☐☐ **Call** me **up** as soon as you arrive.
（你一到就馬上打電話給我。）

☐☐ He has just **hung up**.（他剛掛斷電話。）

實況生活 ❺ ── 談生意用電話洽商

☐☐ I must talk to your boss **right away**.
（我必須馬上和你老闆講話。）

◆ 洽商面談

☐☐ I am sorry **to have kept** you **waiting**.
（很抱歉讓您久等。）

☐☐ I **am with** TTV.（我在台視服務。）

☐☐ I have to **set up** a budget for sales promotion.
（我必須建立預算以推廣銷路。）

☐☐ Please **make yourself comfortable**.
（請不要拘束。）

☐☐ Let me **get the things straight**.
（讓我直言。）

☐☐ Let us **go into details** next time.
（下次讓我們討論詳細情形。）

◆ 找工作

☐☐ It is hard to **find a job**.
（找份工作很難。）

☐☐ Seniority **goes hand in hand** with experience.
（年資與經歷是並進的。）

◆ 應用會話①

A : Hello.　This is Bob.　Who's this？

　　喂，我是鮑伯，請問您是哪一位？

B : This is me — Susie.　我是蘇西。

A : Is your mother at home？　妳媽在家嗎？

B : Yes, she is.　Do you want to talk to her？

　　在，你要跟她說話嗎？

A : Yes, if she isn't tied up.　是的，如果她有空的話。

C : Hello, Bob.　How are you？　喂，鮑伯，你好嗎？

A : Fine, thank you.　How about you？

　　好，謝謝，妳呢？

C : We're all fine.　Dad's awfully busy.　He's writing a book on Taiwan.

　　我們都很好。爸爸十分忙碌，他正在寫一本有關台灣的書。

A : No！　I'd like to read it someday.

　　真的嗎？改天我想拜讀一下。

◆ 應用會話②

A : Hello.　May I speak to Jack？

　　喂，請問傑克在嗎？

B : Speaking！　Hi, Mary.　How are you？

　　我就是！嗨，瑪麗，妳好嗎？

A： I'm fine. Where were you this morning? You missed an important lecture.

我很好。你今早到哪兒去啦？你錯過一堂重要的課了。

B： I had an appointment with the dentist. Had a toothache last night.

我和牙醫有個約會，昨晚鬧牙疼。

A： Oh? Are you all right now?

噢？那你現在還好嗎？

B： Uh-huh. What did the professor say about finals?

嗯。有關期末考的事情，教授說了些什麼？

A： Nothing — except that one question may come out of to-day's lecture.

沒什麼——但有一題問題會出自今天的課。

B： No kidding. I hope you took good notes this morning.

沒開玩笑吧！我希望你今早的筆記好好做。

A： Do you want them tonight?

你今晚想要它們嗎？

B： I sure do. 當然我想要。

實況生活 ❻ — 發燒不舒服的時候

一年難得生幾場病，感冒（cold）是最普遍的。人若是不生病的話，往往容易忽略自己的健康、糟蹋自己寶貴的身體。所以，偶爾生場病（get sick, fall ill）是自己的福氣！但是生病的人最需要別人的關懷與照顧，因此您最好學幾句！

◆ 生病

☐☐ You don't **look well**.（你看起來氣色不好。）

☐☐ I think I'm **getting a cold**.（我想我著涼了。）

☐☐ My cough is **getting worse**.
　　（我的咳嗽愈來愈嚴重了。）

◆ 探問病情

☐☐ I **have a fever**.（我發燒了。）

☐☐ I **ache all over**.（我全身疼痛。）

☐☐ Have you **taken** your **temperature**?
　　（你量過體溫了嗎？）

☐☐ Has the fever **gone down**?（燒退了嗎？）

☐☐ I **have to** take two pills every six hours.
　　（我必須每六小時服兩顆藥丸。）

實況生活 ❻ ── 發燒不舒服的時候

□□ **Take good care of yourself.**
（好好照顧自己。）

□□ I'm **getting better** every day.（我日漸康復。）

◆ 病床閒話

□□ He is **half paralyzed** because of apoplexy.
（他因中風而半身不遂。）

□□ There's no **specific cure** for the AIDS disease.
（沒有治療愛滋病的特效藥。）

□□ The doctor told me to **stay in bed.**
（醫生叫我待在床上。）

□□ Many people **got sick** with the flu.
（許多人得了感冒。）

□□ I **got over** the cold.
（我的感冒好了。）

□□ She is **suffering from** influenza.
（她受感冒的折磨。）

□□ I have **recovered from** my bad cold.
（我從重感冒中復元了。）

❖ 應用會話

A： Could I see Dr. Thomas? I have an appointment for eleven. 我可以見湯瑪斯醫生嗎？我跟他定了11點的約會。

B： Will you come this way, please?
　　請這邊走。

C： What's troubling you? 你出了什麼毛病啦？

A： I've had a terrible headache since early this morning.
　　從今天一大早開始，我就頭疼得厲害。

C： Do you have a fever? 你有發燒嗎？

A： No, I don't. 沒有。

C： How's your appetite? Let me feel your pulse and have a look at your tongue, please.
　　胃口怎麼樣？請讓我量量你的脈搏，看看你的舌頭。

A： Is anything wrong with me?
　　我是怎麼了？

C： Yes. You have a slight cold. As you know, there are a lot of colds going around.
　　你患了輕微的感冒，你知道的，現在感冒正在到處流行。

落下是 **fall**,
陷入情網是 **fall**,
入眠也是 **fall**。
容易入睡爲 " **He falls asleep easily.** "
不容易入睡的人，可說：" **I have a hard time falling asleep.** "

He fell in love with her.

從樓梯掉下來時，也可用 **fall**。
轉爲抽象性的意思，在提到墮落時，也用 **fall**。
墮落天使爲 " **fallen angel** "，另外也有 " **street girl** " 的意思，所以要注意。

He fell down the stairs.

講到「著迷」時，和 **for** 一起，便成 **fall for**。
如果是 **slang** 時，也有逮捕、被檢舉的意思。

He falls for her.

實況生活 ❼ ——情感溝通的表露

外國人的情緒流露（emotional expression）是熱情有勁之外，外加嗓門兒大。有老外在的場合，通常都是 Hi 來 Hi 去之聲不絕於耳，中國人想學好英語，要注意將適當的情緒加入言語之間。

◆ 驚喜

☐☐ How pretty！（好漂亮！）

☐☐ Excellent！Wonderful！（好極了！太好了！）

☐☐ Well done！（做得好！）

☐☐ What a beautiful view！（好美的景色！）

☐☐ I'm glad to hear that．（我很高興聽到那消息。）

◆ 悲歎

☐☐ I'm sorry to hear that．（我很難過聽到那消息。）

☐☐ Alas！（天哪！）

☐☐ That's really too bad！（那真是太糟了！）

☐☐ **I am astounded** by the news．（我被那消息嚇呆了。）

◆ 令人難以置信

☐☐ Oh, dear！（噢，不得了！）

實況生活 ❼ ——情感溝通的表露

☐☐ Really？（是眞的嗎？）

☐☐ Congratulations！（恭喜！）

☐☐ I couldn't believe my eyes.（眞不可思議。）

◆ 費疑猜

☐☐ Well, **let me see**.（嗯，讓我想想看。）

☐☐ Is that so？（是那樣嗎？）

☐☐ Of course.（當然了。）

☐☐ Oh, I see.（噢，我懂了。）

☐☐ You don't say so！（是眞的嗎？）

☐☐ Perhaps so.（大概如此。）

☐☐ It's quite possible.（很有可能。）

◆ 不解人意

☐☐ I beg your pardon？（對不起，請再講一遍。）

☐☐ I'm sorry I can't get you.（對不起，我不懂你的意思。）

☐☐ Would you mind **saying that again**？（請再説一遍好嗎？）

☐☐ Do you get me now？（現在你懂了嗎？）

◆ 不在乎

☐☐ I don't **give a damn**.（我不在乎。）

☐☐ He doesn't have any **sense of guilt**.（他一點也不內疚。）

☐☐ That is **not much of a** thing.（那沒什麼大不了的事。）

◆ 應用會話

A： Surprise！ 給你一個驚喜！

B： Hi, Jimmy. 嗨，吉米。

A： Happy Birthday！ Here. My present.
　　生日快樂！這是我的禮物。

B： Oh, Jimmy. Thank you very much. Come in.
　　噢，吉米，謝謝你。請進。

A： Where is everybody？ 其他人都在哪兒？

B： What do you mean, "Where is everybody?"？
　　你說「其他人都在哪兒」是什麼意思啊？

A： Oh, I guess I′m the first.
　　噢，我以爲我是第一個到的。

B： You mean...？ 你是指…？

A： I mean you′re having a birthday party. Ask your mom.
　　我是指你正要舉行一個慶生會，問問你媽就知道了。

C： That′s right, dear. Happy Birthday！
　　是的，親愛的，生日快樂！

A： Gee！ What an amazing development！
　　噫！那眞是令人驚奇！

hangover 是什麼意思呢?這是喝酒後,身體不舒服,所謂的宿醉。

hangdog 則指「低賤」的意思。

"I've got a hangover."

還有,「電話不要掛斷」,是 "Don't hang up." 這句話是因為以前電話都掛在牆壁上,而流傳下來的話。

hang back 是「躊躇不前」,如: "We hung back as we didn't want to be the first speaker at the meeting."

還有 "Don't keep him hanging, give him an answer." 意思是「不要急,給他一個答案。」

"Hold on, don't hang up!"

"Hang on!" "Hang in there!" 是激勵人的話,意思是「再加一點油,還沒有」。美國人則常和 "Hold on!" 一起使用。

"Hang on!"

實況生活 ❽ ── 怎樣跟別人説 "Hi"

一般人最常碰到的外國人是傳教士（ priest ），他們劈頭就説 " How do you do ? "因此，這句打招呼的話，也成爲大多數台灣人説英語的開場白。

◈ 見面打招呼

☐☐ How do you do？（你好嗎？）

☐☐ Nice to meet you.（很高興見到你。）

☐☐ Pleased to meet you.（很高興見到你。）

☐☐ It's my pleasure.（這是我的榮幸。）

☐☐ How are you **get**ting **along**？（你過得如何？）

☐☐ How is your family？（你家人可好？）

☐☐ As usual.（老樣子。）

◈ 道別

☐☐ See you later.（待會兒見。）

☐☐ So long.（再見。）

☐☐ Well, I must **be off** now.（嗯，我現在必須走了。）

☐☐ Please **remember me to** your family.（請代我向你家人問安。）

❖ 應用會話①

A：Mary, I want you to meet my roommate, Tom.
　　瑪麗，請來見見我的室友湯姆。

B：How do you do, Tom?
　　湯姆，你好。

C：How do you do, Mary? I'm glad to see you.
　　瑪麗，妳好。很高興認識妳。

❖ 應用會話②

A：Hello, George. What's new? 嗨，喬治，過得好嗎？

B：Nothing **in particular**. **How about** you?
　　還是老樣子，你呢？

A：Just the same. How's your wife? 也照舊，你太太好嗎？

B：She is **as** cheerful **as ever**. 她身體和以前一樣好。

❖ 應用會話③

A：Good afternoon, Mrs. Johnson. How are you today?
　　午安，強生太太，今天好嗎？

B：Fine, thank you, and you?
　　好啊，謝謝。你呢？

A：So, so. It's very hot today, isn't it?
　　馬馬虎虎。今天天氣很熱，不是嗎？

PART 3

分秒必爭記憶法

每個時刻，都令人難以忘懷！

●**分秒必爭記憶法的內容**── 有關時間的表達法，天天
用得上，卻常常容易忘，
本單元特羅列比較 time
和 day 的多種用法，使您
醍醐灌頂，迅速吸收。

特色── 分解時間的各種意義，引
伸句型，發展成生活中人
人脫口而出的句子，採條
列式編排，清爽悅目。

目的── 在最短的時間內，掌握時
間片語的用法。

要訣── 善用時空，運用實例，將
時間用法各個擊破。

1. Time的用法

時間就是金錢

—— 時間是很容易消逝的，然而我們並不覺得，一旦半路上遇見一個久未相逢的朋友，這時我們都會有一種「大江東去」的感覺。快節奏的現代社會中，懂得掌握時間是最大的智慧。

看看 Time 的用法！

1. 當「**時間；閒暇**」解

   例：I have no time to read it.（我沒有時間讀它。）

2. 當「**特定時刻；良機**」解

   例：It is the time for you to act.（這是你行動的良機。）

3. 當「**時代**（常用 *pl.*）」解

   例：He was the wisest man of ancient times.

   （他是古代最有識之士。）

4. 當「**次；倍；乘**」解

   例：I called him two times a week.（我一星期打二次電話給他。）

英諺上說：

　"*Time flies .*" ⇨ 光陰如梭。

　"*Time and tide wait for no man .*" ⇨ 歲月不饒人。

現代人說：

　"*Time is money.*" ⇨ 時間就是金錢。

　"*Practice makes perfect.*" ⇨ 熟能生巧。

以下就讓我們來練習—Time 的說法！

時間就是金錢：Time的用法

□□ have a big time 玩得很開心
□□ have a busy time 過一段忙碌時刻
□□ have a time 有麻煩
□□ behind time 遲到
□□ be behind the times 落伍；過時
□□ kill time 消磨時間
□□ mark time 中止；等待
□□ on time 準時

□□ time and again 反覆
□□ time after time 再三；屢次不斷
□□ times are good（bad） 景氣好（壞）
□□ take time out 休息
□□ take time 不慌不忙

□□ at times 有時；間或
□□ at a time 一次
□□ at the time 當時
□□ at all times 時常
□□ by the time 頃刻之間
□□ by this time 在這時候
□□ in time 及時
□□ in time for（to） 適時地
□□ in time of need 窮困時

時間就是金錢：Time的用法

☐☐ **against time** 定時限；盡快地

☐☐ **all in good time** 時機一到；等候時機

☐☐ **all the time** 老是

☐☐ **do time** 〔俗〕服刑

☐☐ **for a time** 一時

☐☐ **for the time being** 暫時

☐☐ **from time to time** 時常

☐☐ **give time** 寬限時日

☐☐ **in bad times** 誤時

☐☐ **in good times** 適時

☐☐ **in no time** 立卽

☐☐ **of the time** 當時

☐☐ **on** *one's* **own time** 無報酬

☐☐ **out of time** 不合時宜

☐☐ **serve** *one's* **time** 當學徒

☐☐ **some time or other** 遲早

☐☐ **tell the time** 報時

♧ When did she get married?
她什麼時候結婚的？

2. Day的用法
掌握現在就是掌握永遠

—— 你看過「屋頂上的提琴手」這部電影嗎？或者您聽過 " Sun rise, sun set." 這首歌嗎？劇中那一對夫妻便感傷地唱起 " （男）Is this the little girl I carried？ Is this the little boy at play？（女）I don't remember growing older day by day." 看完這一段後，相信您會體會「一日又一日」的感覺了。

溫習一下 day 的用法！

1. 表「**一日，一晝夜**」

　例：Take a day off！（休息一天。）

2. 表「**白天，晝**」

　例：We'll arrive there before day.（我們會在天亮前抵達。）

3. 表「**一生活動的全盛時期**（常用 *pl*.）」

　例：(1) Old Sam ended his days.（老山姆去世了。）

　　　(2) Our day is gone.（我們的時代過去了。）

4. 表「**每日的工作時數**」

　例：They want a six-hour day and a five-day week.

　　　（他們要求每日工作六小時，每週五天。）

要不要試看看您對 day 的瞭解程度呢？下面有二個例句：

　⇨ She lives *to this day*.（她活到現在。）

　⇨ She is ninety *if a day*.（如果沒錯的話，她已九十歲了。）

怎樣，至少您猜對了一半 !?

　繼續，來看看 day 還有什麼說法！

掌握現在就是掌握永遠：Day 的用法

☐☐ **day in** 一天來了
☐☐ **day out** 一天過去了
☐☐ **day off** 休息一天
    have a day off
    take a day off
    give a day off
☐☐ **some day** 將來有一天
☐☐ **to this day** 活到現在

☐☐ **the day after today** 明天
☐☐ **the day after tomorrow** 後天
☐☐ **the day before yesterday** 前天
☐☐ **day and night** 日以繼夜
☐☐ **day by day** 日復一日
☐☐ **from day to day** 一日之間
☐☐ **by day** 日間
☐☐ **by the day** 按日計算
    by the month 按月計算
    by the hour 按時計算

掌握現在就是掌握永遠：Day 的用法

☐☐ **day is done** 已成過去；完結

☐☐ (*one's*) **day is over**
(人的輝煌時期)過去；完結

☐☐ **all day long** 終日

☐☐ **call it a day** 〔俗〕今天到此
為止

☐☐ **carry the day** 得勝

☐☐ **day about** 隔日

☐☐ **have** *one's* **day** 走運；得意

☐☐ **if a day** 確實；不錯

☐☐ **in a day** 一日之內

☐☐ **in days gone by** 過去

☐☐ **in days to come** 將來

☐☐ **in** *one's* **day**
在人年靑(旺盛)時

☐☐ **of the day** 現今的

☐☐ **this day week** 上週的今天

☐☐ **to a day** 一天都不差；正巧

Mama Has Much Hair

    Jim： "Mama, why doesn't papa have any hair?"

Mother： "Because he thinks so much, dear."

    Jim： "Why do you have so much hair, then?"

Mother： "Because — but, ***go away*** and do your

        lessons."

媽媽頭髮多

吉姆：「媽媽，爸爸為什麼一根頭髮也沒有呢？」

媽媽：「因為他頭腦好啊，親愛的。」

吉姆：「那麼，為什麼你的頭髮這麼多呢？」

媽媽：「因為——嗯，**走開**去做你的功課。」

3. 表期間、時刻的用法
享受精朵的時段

—— 在英語世界的生活中，我們會經常問人家時刻，像「何時回來呀？」「準備待多久啊？」，或者人家問我們也一樣，都需要給予對方一個較清楚的概念及回答，您要如何說呢？

看看有關表示期間、時刻的用法！

1. 表示特定次數

例：(1) How often do you see John？（你多久見約翰一次面？）

⇨ I see him every other day.（兩天見一次。）

(2) How many times a month do you write letters？
（你一個月寫幾次信？）

⇨ I write twice a month.（我一個月寫兩次。）

2. 表示特定的一段時間

例：How long did you wait？（你等多久了？）

⇨ I waited for half an hour.（半個小時。）

3. 表示含糊的一段時間

例：How long did you stay abroad？（你在國外待多久？）

⇨ I stayed for a little while.（只待了一下子。）

4. 表示非限定的回數

例：I went home by bus most of the time.
（我大部份時間都搭公車回家。）

接下來，有許多表示一段時刻的用語，請您來熟記！

享受精采的時段：表期間、時刻的用法

① 表特定的時刻、期間

☐☐ **for the time being**	暫時
☐☐ **for the next few days**	未來幾天
☐☐ **during the past two weeks**	過去兩週之間
☐☐ **all this week**	本週一週；整個禮拜
☐☐ **all last month**	上個月整月
☐☐ **all next year**	明年全年
☐☐ **all day long yesterday**	昨天一整天
☐☐ **all last night**	昨夜一整夜
☐☐ **since last year**	自去年以來
☐☐ **until noon**	直到中午

② 表示含糊的一段時間

☐☐ **for a little while**	暫時
☐☐ **for a long time**	有很長的時間了
☐☐ **as long as possible**	時間愈長愈好；儘可能的久
☐☐ **for ages**	長時間

③ 表一段時間

☐☐ **for ten minutes**	十分鐘
☐☐ **for half an hour**	半小時
☐☐ **an hour and a half**	一小時半
☐☐ **a couple of months**	兩個月
☐☐ **a quarter of an hour**	一刻鐘；十五分鐘
☐☐ **three quarters of an hour**	四十五分鐘

享受精采的時段：表期間、時刻的用法

④ 表示特定的次數

☐☐ **once a day** 一天一次

☐☐ **every afternoon** 每天下午

☐☐ **every other day** 每隔一天

☐☐ （**once**）**every 5 minutes** 每五分鐘（一回）

☐☐ **twice a week** 一週兩次

☐☐ **every hour on the hour** 每一時的整個小時

☐☐ **every Friday morning** 每個禮拜五的早上

☐☐ **every six months** 每半年

☐☐ **annually** 每年

☐☐ **weekly** 每週

☐☐ **daily** 每日

⑤ 其他表示次數的方法

☐☐ **once in a while** 偶爾

☐☐ **off and on** 斷斷續續

☐☐ **every now and then** 有時

☐☐ **no more often than necessary** 時常需要的

☐☐ **more often than not** 時常

☐☐ **as often as possible** 盡可能每次都～

☐☐ **most of the time** 大部份時間

♣ How long did you wait? 你等多久了?

♣ How long did you stay abroad? 你在國外待多久?

4. 數量名詞的用法
精打細算不吃虧

—— 英語中，數量名詞的用法也很重要，像生活中你不可以說：
" Please give me two papers." 而應該說：" Please give
me *two sheets of* paper." 中文裏，也有許多各種不同的
數量稱呼，如「一個人」、「兩張紙」、「三枝筆」等，
因為物質名詞是不可數名詞，前面不可有不定冠詞和數詞！

溫習一下數量名詞的基本用法！

1. 以容器來表單位

例： a cup of coffee 　　（一杯咖啡）

　　 a glass of water 　　（一杯水）

　　 a bowl of rice 　　（一碗飯）

2. 以形狀來表單位

例： a piece of paper 　　（一張紙）

　　 a piece of bread 　　（一塊麵包＜用手撕開的一小塊＞）

　　 a slice of bread 　　（一片麵包）

3. 以度、量、衡為單位

例： a pound of beef 　　　（一磅牛肉）

　　 a catty of beef 　　　（一斤牛肉）

　　 a gallon of gasoline 　（一加侖汽油）

　　 a foot of snow 　　　（一呎深的雪）

底下有十種常用的數量單位用法，請看！

精打細算不吃虧：數量名詞的用法

□□ **a piece of**　一個（塊）～

a piece of bread	（一片麵包）
a piece of paper	（一張紙）
a piece of furniture	（一件傢俱）
a piece of mail	（一封信）
a piece of advice	（一個忠告）
a piece of cloth	（一匹布）
a piece of cheese	（一塊乳酪）
a piece of sugar	（一塊方糖）
a piece of chocolate	（一塊巧克力）
a piece of meat	（一片肉）
a piece of cabbage	（一顆甘藍菜）
a piece of lettuce	（一顆萵苣）

□□ **a gallon of**　一加侖～

a gallon of oil , gasoline	（一加侖油，汽油）

□□ **a bottle of**　一瓶～

a bottle of beer	（一瓶啤酒）
whiskey, milk	（威士忌酒，牛奶）

□□ **a cup of**（**a glass of**）一杯～

a cup of coffee	（一杯咖啡）
a glass of juice	（一杯果汁）

□□ **a bar of**　一條～

a bar of soap	（一條肥皂）

精打細算不吃虧：數量名詞的用法

☐☐ **a pound of** 一磅～

    a pound of beef   （一磅牛肉）

    a pound of mutton   （一磅羊肉）

    a pound of ham   （一磅火腿）

☐☐ **a head of** 一顆～

    a head of lettuce   （一顆萵苣）

    a head of cabbage   （一顆甘藍菜）

☐☐ **a slice of** 一片～

    a slice of ham   （一片火腿）

    a slice of bread   （一片麵包）

☐☐ **a gust of** 一陣～

    a gust of wind   （一陣風）

☐☐ **an ear of** 一根～

    an ear of corn   （一根玉蜀黍）

● 容易誤譯的慣用語 ●

以下為您介紹在翻譯時，容易被誤譯的片語，請先逐次譯出（口譯或筆譯皆可）以下句子，再對照答案，將錯誤的地方多讀幾次，以便牢記。

1. He is a man *after my own heart*.
2. I always *enjoy your company*.
3. The earthquake took place *before my time*.
4. He was born *before his name*.
5. Don't *carry coals to New Castle*.
6. They *buried the hatchet*（斧）and went home happily.
7. Did you believe the *cock-and-bull story* he told us?
8. The teacher gave her *a dirty look*.
9. You must *face the music*.
10. Tom *has a lot on the ball*.

《解答》

1. 恰合我心意
2. 很樂於和你在一起
3. 在我出生前
4. 早產
5. 白費力氣（New Castle 是煤的產地）
6. 言歸於好
7. 無聊的話
8. 露出不快的表情（不要誤譯為討厭的眼神）
9. 不怕承擔困難
10. 有能力

PART 4

熱門動詞記憶法
作秀頻率高，效用最大！

● **熱門動詞記憶法的內容**——　篩選出現頻率最高，看似
簡單卻最容易搞混的 12 個
動詞，所組成的動詞片語。

特色——　由 12 個基本動詞衍生出千
變萬化的動詞片語，您只
要按字母順序熟記片語，
就能完全區分動詞用法，
隨心所欲。

目的——　動詞在整個英文句子中，
有著牽一髮而動全身的重
要性，12 個動詞，能為您
打下一口流利的會話基礎，
不費吹灰之力。

要訣——　先充分認清每個動詞的意
義，再熟記它加了哪些東
西，才成為動詞片語。巧
用聯想力，從趣味中理解
之。

1. Be 動詞
學好英文的第一步

—— 提到 " be " 動詞，就使我們聯想到從國中開始學英文，就是從 " I am a boy (girl). " 開始，直到今天， " be " 動詞和我們已結下了不解之緣。

複習 be 動詞的用法！

be 動詞可當做：1. 連綴動詞　2. 完全不及物動詞　3. 助動詞

① 當做**連綴動詞**（ linking verb ），用來連接主詞和述詞。作用相當於不完全不及物動詞。

　　如：(1) I am he. （我即是他。）

　　　　(2) This is great. （這太棒了。）

　　　　(3) Four times two is eight. （四乘二是八。）

② 當做**完全不及物動詞**，表「存在」，「在」的意思。

　　如：(1) God is. （上帝存在。）

　　　　(2) I was there. （我在那裏。）

③ 當做**助動詞**（ auxiliary ），以造成進行式（ progressive tense ）和被動語態（ passive voice ）。

　　如：(1) John is waiting for you. （約翰在等你。）

　　　　(2) This cup has been washed. （這只杯子已被洗過。）

　　另外，| **be 動詞＋to 不定詞** | ，表示未來。

　　如：(1) Tom is to meet Mary here.（湯姆將在此地和瑪莉見面。）

　　　　(2) The show was to begin today. （這齣戲將在今天開始。）

以下就從日常生活最常用的 be 動詞開始！

學好英文的第一步：Be動詞片語

◆ 生活中最常用 be 動詞片語

☐☐ **be sure to V** 務必；一定；確定

›→ **Be sure to** come home early today.
　　今天一定要早點回家。

›→ **Be sure to** pass the exams.
　　務必要通過考試。

›→ **Be sure to** be in time.
　　一定要及時到達。

›→ **Be sure** not **to** eat too much.
　　確定不要吃太多東西。

☐☐ **be able to V** 能夠

›→ Will you **be able to** see him?
　　你能夠去看他嗎?

›→ I'm sure I'll **be able to** find it.
　　我確信能夠找到它。

☐☐ **be glad to V** 高興

›→ I'm **glad to** hear that she is unmarried.
　　我很高興聽到她還沒結婚。

›→ I'm **glad to** say that the boss has been very well lately.
　　我很高興地說老闆最近非常好。

☐☐ **be supposed to V** 應該；應當

›→ I **am supposed to** go to New York next week.
　　下禮拜我應當到紐約。

›→ He **is supposed to** be at home today.
　　今天他應該在家。

學好英文的第一步：Be動詞片語

☐ be interested in 對～感到興趣

　» Everybody **was interested in** the story.
　　每個人都對這故事感到興趣。

☐ be through with 完畢；結束

　» **Are** you **through with** the phone？
　　你電話講完了嗎？

　» I'm **through with** her.
　　我和她吹了。

☐ be known to 爲～所知

　» He **is known to** everybody.
　　他是衆所周知的人物。（ Everybody knows him. ）

☐ be known by 因～才知道；辨識出

　» A man **is known by** the company he keeps.
　　什麼樣的朋友，什麼樣的人。

　» I **know** you **by** name.
　　我只知道你的名字。

☐ be good for 適用

　» What **is** this medicine
　　good for？
　　這種藥適用於什麼症狀？

　» This medicine **is good**
　　for a cold.
　　這種藥適用於感冒。

學好英文的第一步：Be動詞片語

◆ 按字母順序熟記be動詞片語

☐☐ **be able to V** 能夠

⇨ Will you be able to come tomorrow?
你明天能來嗎？

☐☐ **be about to V** 即將

⇨ He was about to start. 他即將出發。

☐☐ **be absorbed in** 全神貫注

☐☐ **be accompanied by** 陪伴；跟隨

☐☐ **be accompanied with** 附上～；伴以～

⇨ All orders must be accompanied with cash.
所有訂單必須附上現金。

☐☐ **be acquainted with** 知曉的

⇨ acquaint ＋人＋ with 介紹；使認識

☐☐ **be afraid of** 害怕（ be afraid to V 害怕去做）

⇨ He is afraid of swimming. 他怕游泳。

⇨ He is afraid to swim. 他害怕去游泳。

☐☐ **be alive to** 對～敏感；察覺；曉得

☐☐ **be alive with** 充滿（活的或動的東西）

☐☐ **be anxious about** 擔心～

⇨ I am anxious about the result. 我擔心結果。

☐☐ **be anxious for ＋N**，**be anxious to ＋V** 渴望

⇨ He is anxious to know the result. 他渴望知道結果。

學好英文的第一步：Be動詞片語

□□ **be apt to V** 有～傾向

　　⇨ He is apt to forget. 他有健忘的傾向。

□□ **be aware of, be aware to** 知道～

　　　反 be blinded to 對～缺乏判斷力

　　　反 be blinded by（with）爲～所蒙蔽

□□ **be bare of** 赤裸的；沒有～的

　　⇨ The hill is bare of trees. 這山沒有樹木。

□□ **be bereaved of** 剝奪；喪失

　　⇨ She was bereaved of a son. 她喪失一個兒子。

　　＊ bereave A of B 從A（sb.）剝奪B（sb. or sth.）

□□ **be busy** 忙的；勤勉的；繁華的

□□ **be capable of** 勝任～

□□ **be careful of** 謹愼～　同 take good care of 好好照顧

□□ **be careful about**（in, with）關心；注意

□□ **be careful to V** 小心；注意　反 be careless of 粗心大意

　　⇨ Be careful not to break it. 小心不要打破！

□□ **be convinced of** 使信服

□□ **be crowded with** 擠滿人的；因～擁擠

　　⇨ The store was crowded with holiday shoppers.
　　　這家店擠滿了假日購物的人潮。

學好英文的第一步：Be動詞片語

☐☐ **be delighted〔pleased, glad〕to V〔with, at〕** 欣然～；樂於～

⇨ I was delighted to hear the news.

　　我聽到這消息極為高興。

☐☐ **be depended on** 依賴～

⇨ He is a man that can be depended on. 他是一個可依賴的男人。

* depend on A（*sb.* or *sth.*）for B（*sth.*）

　　依賴A的支持，B方可存在，成為事實。

· He depends on his pen for a living. 他靠寫作為生。

☐☐ **be determined to V** 決定去做～

⇨ I am determined to go there. 我決定到那裏去。

☐☐ **be due to**

　　（＋N.）應歸於～

⇨ For my success my thanks are due to you.

　　至於我的成功我的感謝都應歸於你。

　　（＋V.）預定的

⇨ I am due to speak tonight. 今晚我預定發表談話。

☐☐ **be engaged in** 忙～；從事於～

同 be occupied in

☐☐ **be familiar with** 熟悉～；精通～

⇨ I am familiar with your name.

　　我熟悉您的大名。

☐☐ **be famous for** 以～出名

學好英文的第一步：Be動詞片語

□□ **be filled with** 充滿～；填滿～

＊ fill A with B → 使A填滿B

・ They filled a hole with sand. 他們用沙填滿了一個洞。

□□ **be fond of** 喜愛～；喜歡～

⇨ He is very fond of music. 他非常喜歡音樂。

□□ **be going to V** 將要；正打算

⇨ I am going to see him today. 今天我將要去見他。

□□ **be good for** 有益於～

□□ **be good at** 善於

⇨ She is good at painting. 她善於繪畫。

□□ **be inferior to** 劣等的；下級的

反 be superior to 上等的；比～好的

□□ **be interested in** 對～有興趣

□□ **be known to** 熟悉～　＊ be known by 因～辨認出

□□ **be made up of** 由～組成　同 consists of

□□ **be pleased with（at）** 對～表示高興；樂於～

⇨ I am pleased at your coming. 我對你的到來表示高興。

＊ be pleased to do 喜歡（做）～

□□ **be present at** 出席

□□ **be proof against** 抵抗

⇨ She is proof against any temptation. 她能抵抗一切的誘惑。

學好英文的第一步：Be動詞片語

☐☐ **be proud of** 對～感到驕傲

☐☐ **be quick at**（**of, to V**）敏捷的；迅速的

　　⇨ Quick at meal, quick at work. 趕快吃飯，趕快做事。

　　反 **be slow to** 動作慢的

☐☐ **be ready for** 準備～

　　＊ be ready to V 隨時可以去～

☐☐ **be rich in** 富饒於～

☐☐ **be subject to** 使蒙受～；應服從的～；易受～

☐☐ **be sure to V** 必然

　　⇨ He is sure to succeed. 他必然會成功。

☐☐ **be tired of** 厭倦

　　⇨ I am tired of hearing it. 我厭倦聽訟。

☐☐ **be tired with** 疲倦

　　⇨ I am tired with long work. 長久的工作使我感到疲倦。

☐☐ **be true to** 忠實的

　　＊ be true of ～適用於～

☐☐ **be used to** 習慣於

　　同 be accustomed to

☐☐ **be wanting in** 缺乏

　　同 be lacking in

　　⇨ He is wanting in common sense.

　　　他缺乏常識。

2. Do動詞

打好英文基礎的尖兵

—— 前項所講的 be 動詞，是對狀態和存在的表示，do 則可說是指示動作的動詞。

溫習一下 do 的用法！

do 可作為： 1. 助動詞　2. 主要動詞

1. 助動詞

(1) 使主要動詞完成疑問與否定形式。

如：I know John. ⇨ **Do you** know John ?

I like snakes. ⇨ I **don′t** like snakes.

(2) 用於「附加問句」，「簡答句」中，代替主要動詞。

如：You know Michael, don′t you ?

A：He plays football.　　B：So do I.

(3) 用於肯定句中，表示強調與說服。

如：**Do** sit down.

You **do** look nice today.

(4) 用於倒裝句中，強調置於句首的副詞。

如：At no time **did** he lose his temper.

2. 主要動詞

在疑問句與否定句中，do 可以重覆使用：一為主要動詞，一為助動詞。

如：① When **do** you **do** your homework ?
　　　　　助動詞　　主要動詞

② We **don′t do** much work on Saturday.
　　　助動詞　　主要動詞

讓我們繼續下去學 do 的用語！

打好英文基礎的尖兵 ： Do 動詞片語

◆ 利用生活慣用的 do 片語來學習！

□□ **do by** 待（人）

➻ She **did** well **by** him.

　　她待他好。

□□ **done** 煮；烹調

➻ Is this steak **done**? Yes, it′s well-done.

　　這塊牛排煎好了嗎？是的，已經煎得很熟了。

□□ **done for** 完蛋

➻ I′m **done for**.

　　我完蛋了。

□□ **do for** 做；實行

➻ I will **do** anything **for** you.

　　我會為你做任何事情。

□□ **do good business** 生意興隆

➻ The Commercial Bank is **doing good business**.

　　商業銀行生意興旺。

囡 The business is slow. 生意不景氣。

□□ **to do** 去做～；幹事

➻ Don′t you have anything **to do**?

　　你沒事幹嗎？

□□ **do without** 免除；不用

➻ Can you **do without** smoking for a week?

　　你能一個禮拜不抽煙嗎？

打好英文基礎的尖兵：Do 動詞片語

◈ 按字母順序來學 do 的說法！

☐☐ **do away with** 廢除；放棄

　　回 get rid of 免除　　回 give up 放棄

☐☐ **do for** 適合～之用；致死；毀掉；使失敗；照料

☐☐ **do good** 爲善

☐☐ **do wrong** 做錯事；做壞事

☐☐ **do＋人＋good** 對～人有益　　図 do＋人＋harm 對～人造成傷害

　　＊ do＋人＋a good turn 施惠於人；行善事於人

　　＊ do＋人＋wrong 對人誤解

　　・ You did me wrong. 你誤解我了。

☐☐ **do justice to** 對～公平對待

　　＊ to do＋人＋justice 給予～人公平

☐☐ **do much for** 有貢獻

　　⇨ He has done much for his company.

　　　他對他的公司貢獻很大。

☐☐ **do＋人＋a favor** 施恩～人；幫忙～人

　　⇨ Do me the favor to come. 幫幫忙一定要來。

☐☐ **do *one's* best** 盡力而爲

☐☐ **do *one's* part** 盡義務　　＊ do well by 對～有助益

☐☐ **do with** 需要；利用；忍受

　　⇨ What shall I do with it？我要怎樣處理它？

　　＊ have much to do with 與～大有關係

　　＊ have done with 完成；辦完；與～斷絕關係

Polite but Not Kind

A stranger ***called at*** a house in a long street, and asked the maid who opened the door:

" Does Mr. Smith live here?"

" No, sir," was her polite reply.

" Does he ***live in*** this street?" asked the stranger.

" Yes, sir."

" Do you know his number?" asked the stranger.

" No, sir, but you will find it on his door."

禮貌却不親切

陌生人**拜訪**長街上的一間房子，並問來開門的女僕說：

「史密斯先生住這兒嗎？」

「不，先生，」她禮貌地回答。

「他**住在**這條街嗎？」陌生人問道。

「是的，先生。」

「妳知道他住幾號嗎？」陌生人問。

「不知道，先生，但你可以在他的門上找到。」

3.Have動詞
奠定英文實力的基石

—— 我們都知道 have 是「擁有」的意思，如 I have a book.
（我有一本書。）I have an appointment。（我有個約會。）但
是，你知道 Doesn't he have any sense at all？的意思
嗎？欲知答案，請看 have sense！

溫習一下 have 的用法！

以下介紹四種 have 的用法：

1. **表示時間和精神狀態的持續：**

　　如：(1) We had a good time yesterday.（昨天我們玩得很愉快。）

　　　　(2) I have no doubt about it.（對於那件事，我一點也不懷疑。）

2. **have＋名詞：表活動**

　　如：(1) May I have your pen？（鋼筆借一下，可以嗎？）

　　　　(2) We'll have fine weather tomorrow.（明天會是好天氣。）

　　　　(3) You had a call from Mr. Lin.（林先生打電話來找你。）

　　　　(4) Would you like to have something to drink？
　　　　　　（要不要喝點什麼？）

3. **had better＋原形動詞：最好做～**

　　如：You had better go with him.（你最好和他一起去。）

4. **have to：表義務**

　　如：(1) You don't have to go.（你不用去。）

　　　　(2) Do you often have to speak French in your job？
　　　　　　（你工作時得常常說法語嗎？）

接下來熟悉一下 have 的說法！

奠定英文實力的基石：Have 動詞片語

◆ 運用生活中最常用的 have 片語！

☐☐ **have on** 穿上

→ He **has** a blue coat **on**.
　　他穿上一件藍色外套。

☐☐ **have to V** 必須

→ I don't **have to** go — I want to go.
　　我可以不必去，但我想去。

☐☐ **have done with** 完成

→ Let's start at once and **have** it **done with**.
　　讓我們立刻開始並且完成它。

☐☐ **have a cold** 感冒

→ Don't come near me. I **have a cold**.
　　不要靠近我，我感冒了。

☐☐ **have a good time** 享受；玩得愉快

→ Did you **have a good time** this afternoon?
　　今天下午你玩得愉快嗎？

☐☐ **have a heart** 慈悲；同情

→ Oh, **have a heart**.
　　哦，請大發慈悲吧！

☐☐ **have sense** 常識

→ Doesn't he **have** any **sense** at all?
　　難道他一點常識也沒有嗎？

奠定英文實力的基石：Have 的相關片語

◆ 按字母順序來學 have 的說法！

☐☐ **have a chat with** 與人閒聊

☐☐ **have the flu** 感冒

☐☐ **have a credit for** 有～評價（名聲）

　　　＊ have credit for 認為有～功績；credit 加 a, the 是名譽、名聲之意。

☐☐ **have a dislike for** 對～嫌惡

　　　园 have a fancy for 對～喜歡

☐☐ **have a good time** 享受一段快樂時光；過得愉快

☐☐ **have a hard time** 難關　圓 have quite a time

☐☐ **have a heart** 慈悲　园 have no heart 無憐憫之心

☐☐ **have a mind to V** 欲～；頗想～

　　　⇨ I have a mind to accompany him to America.

　　　　我頗想陪他去美國。

☐☐ **have an eye for** 能夠瞭解～

☐☐ **have an eye to** 着眼於～

☐☐ **have an eye on** 注意～；留意看～

☐☐ **have done with** 停止做某事；與～不再有關係

　　　⇨ He is dishonest; I have done with him.

　　　　他不老實，我跟他的關係已結束。

☐☐ **have an effect on** 對～產生效用

☐☐ **have much trouble to V** 費心（力）作

☐☐ **have no business to V** 無做此之權利；無義務去做～

奠定英文實力的基石：Have助開片語

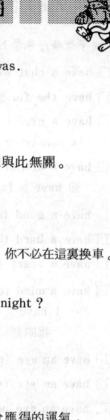

☐☐ **have no idea of** 對～毫無概念

⇨ I had no idea of what the theory was.

我對這理論毫無概念。

☐☐ **have no knowledge of** 對～毫無所知

☐☐ **have nothing to do with** 與～無關

⇨ This has nothing to do with you. 你與此無關。

反 have much to do with 與～大有關係

☐☐ **have something to do with** 與～有關

☐☐ **had better not** 不必

⇨ You had better not change cars here. 你不必在這裏換車。

☐☐ **have on** 穿（衣）；戴（帽）

⇨ What do you have on for tomorrow night ?

你明晚穿什麼服裝？

* have on 指穿著狀態；put on 指穿著動作

☐☐ **have only to V** 即使做～也可以

☐☐ **have** *one's* **share** 應得之分

⇨ He had his share of luck. 他有他一分應得的運氣。

☐☐ **have** *one's* **way** 隨心所欲；爲所欲爲

☐☐ **have** *one's* **say** 與聞；干預；有分

⇨ Let him have his say. 讓他參加一分吧。

☐☐ **have（no）place in** 有（無）～地位；有（無）容身之地

⇨ Envy has no place in his heart. 他無嫉妒之心。

☐☐ **have（no）reason to V** 有（沒有）理由去～

奠定英文實力的基石：Have動用片語

- [ ] **have recourse to** 求助於～

- [ ] **have reference to** 言及；提及

- [ ] **have regard to** 注意；留神　反 have no regard to 不注重
  - ⇨ He has no regard to appearance. 他不注重外表。

- [ ] **have regard for** 尊重；禮遇　反 have no regard for 不尊重
  - * having regard to～ 考慮～

- [ ] **have seen better days** 處境曾經好過；曾經富有過

- [ ] **have the best of it** 勝利
  - 反 have the worst of it 失敗

- [ ] **have the good fortune to V** 走好運
  - ⇨ I had the good fortune to succeed.
    我運氣好而成功。
  - 反 have the ill fortune to V 運氣差

- [ ] **have the goodness to V** 懇請；祈；希
  - ⇨ Have the goodness to answer my letter at your earliest convenience. 請儘早回覆我的信。

- [ ] **have the heart to V** 有勇氣（做某事）

- [ ] **have to V** 必須～（表義務）

- [ ] **have to do with** 與～有關

- [ ] **have words with** 與～爭辯
  - ⇨ If you fiddle with my camera again, I am going to have words with you.
    假如你再摸我的照相機，休怪我與你翻臉。

Why ?

"Why do you *go to bed* at night?"

"Because the bed does not come
to me."

「晚上你為什麼要**上牀**？」

「因為牀不走近我。」

"Why do you carry that stick?"

"Because it can't walk."

「為什麼你拿著那根枴杖？」

「因為枴杖不會走路。」

"Why did you buy that hat?"

"Because I couldn't get it
for nothing."

「你為什麼買那頂帽子？」

「因為我無法**平白**得到它。」

4.Keep動詞
貯蓄英文能源的法寶

── keep 比 have 的「持續時間」長，它含有「保持」與「繼續」某種狀態的意思。若 keep 後面直接接物品的話, 則又有「保藏」、「管理」和「遵守」等意思。如:

① Keep cool！保持冷靜！

② Some people always keep old letters. 有些人愛藏舊信件。

③ I am busy all day keeping house. 我整天忙著料理家務。

④ He is a man who keeps his word. 他是一個守信用的人。

溫習一下 keep 的用法！

以下介紹 keep 的四種用法:

1. **使某人持續某狀態：keep＋受詞＋受詞補語**

   如：(1) I am sorry to have kept you waiting.

   （很抱歉讓您久等。）

   (2) I won't keep you long.（我不會讓您耽擱太久。）

2. **keep＋補語**：表示保持

   如：I'll keep quiet .（我會保持安靜。）

3. **keep A from B**：使 A 不能 B

   如：Please keep her from talking.（請不要讓她說話。）

不管怎樣，將 keep 當做以「維持」為目的的動詞來理解的話，意思自然就很容易明白了，Keep it in mind！

再看看 keep 要怎麼說！

貯蓄英文能源的法寶　Keep 的開片語

◈ 從生活最常用的 keep 動詞學習

☐☐ **keep a secret** 保守秘密

　　➤ Please **keep it a secret**.
　　　　請保守秘密。

　　➤ I **keep** nothing **a secret** from you.
　　　　我沒有隱瞞你甚麼。

☐☐ **keep at** 堅持；不要放棄

　　➤ **Keep at it**!
　　　　不要放棄！

☐☐ **keep an eye on** 照料；照顧

　　➤ **Keep an eye on** the baby for a while.
　　　　請照顧一下孩子。

☐☐ **keep back** 拒絕洩露；藏住

　　➤ I will **keep** nothing **back** from you.
　　　　我對你將毫無隱藏。

☐☐ **keep company with** 與～交往

　　➤ Don't **keep company with** such a man.
　　　　不要跟這種男人交往。

☐☐ **keep house** 做家事；料理家務

　　➤ I'm busy all day **keeping house**.
　　　　我整天忙著做家事。

☐☐ **keep on** 繼續；不斷

　　➤ If you **keep on** drinking like that, you'll get sick.
　　　　你再這樣繼續喝下去，你會生病的。

貯蓄英文能源的法寶：Keep動間片語

☐☐ **keep off** 遠離；離開

　↦ **Keep off** the grass！
　　離開草地！

☐☐ **Keep** *one's* **hands off** 不要動手

　↦ **Keep your hands off** my typewriter.
　　不要碰我的打字機。

☐☐ **keep** *one's* **head** 保持冷靜

　↦ I admire you for **keeping your head.**
　　我羨慕你能夠保持冷靜。

☐☐ **keep** *one's* **seat** 不用讓座

　↦ I'm getting off at the next stop．Please **keep your
　　seat.** *我下一站就下車了，請不用讓座。*

☐☐ **keep** *one's* **word** 遵守諾言

　↦ You will **keep your word,** won't you？
　　你會遵守諾言，是吧！

☐☐ **keep out** 禁止進入

　↦ **Keep out.** *禁止進入！*
　↦ Danger！**Keep out!** *危險！禁止進入！*

☐☐ **keep quiet** 保持安靜

　↦ There is a conference going on in the next room．
　　Let's **keep quiet.**
　　隔壁正在開會，我們保持安靜吧！

☐☐ **keep to the left** 靠左通行

貯蓄英文能源的法寶：Keep 動詞片語

❖ 按字母順序來學 keep 的說法！

☐☐ **keep a secret** 保守秘密　反 let out a secret 洩露秘密

☐☐ **keep accounts** 記帳；管帳

☐☐ **keep at** 堅持；不要放棄

☐☐ **keep ～ at a distance** 保持距離

☐☐ **keep back** 拒絕洩露

☐☐ **keep company with** 交往

☐☐ **keep down** 使（經費等）不增加
　　　　⇨ We must keep down expenses. 我們必須節制開銷。

☐☐ **keep good hours** 早睡早起
　　　　反 keep bad hours 不按時回家、睡覺

☐☐ **keep house** 料理家務；成家

☐☐ **keep the house** 居家不外出

☐☐ **keep ～ in mind** 銘記在心

☐☐ **keep in touch with** 與～保持接觸

☐☐ **keep off** 離開

☐☐ **keep on** 繼續

☐☐ **keep** *one's* **word** 遵守諾言

☐☐ **keep** *one's* **end up** 〔俗〕做好分內工作　同 hold one's end up
　　　　⇨ Mary washed the dishes so fast that Ann, who was
　　　　　　drying them, couldn't keep her end up.
　　　　　　瑪莉洗碗很快，以致擦碗的安工作趕不上。

☐☐ **keep** *one's* **feet** 不跌倒

貯蓄英文能源的法寶：Keep動詞片語

☐☐ **keep** *one's* **head** 冷靜

☐☐ **keep** *one's* **hands off** 不許動手

☐☐ **keep out** 不准進入　＊＋of 避開

☐☐ **keep quiet** 保持安靜

☐☐ **keep silence** 保持沈默　回 break silence 打破沈默

☐☐ **keep silent** 保持無聲的

☐☐ **keep still** 保持不動

⇨ Keep your hands still. 你的手保持不動。

☐☐ **keep time with**（**music**）隨著（音樂）打拍子

☐☐ **keep to** 遵守　＊keep to oneself 保守秘密；不與他人交往

☐☐ **keep up** 繼續下去

⇨ Keep up your courage. 不要氣餒。

☐☐ **keep it up** 照目前的情形繼續下去。

☐☐ **keep up with** 趕上

⇨ We must keep up with the times. 我們必須趕上時代。

☆ keep＋人＋waiting 使（人）等待

（I am sorry to have kept you waiting so long. 很抱歉
讓您久等。）

☆ keep～from＋動名詞　預防；使～免於

（Activity keeps the mind from rusting. 活動使人心智
免於陳腐。）

come up with 想出

come to me 到我這兒來

5. Come動詞

展現英文魅力的尤物

——在英語中，要正確地選擇使用 come 與 go，並不是一件容易的事。一般而言，用 come 的情況，是到說話者或聽話者所在地的動作，如 " Come here ! " 而 go 則表示與此方向相反的動作，如 " Go there "。

熟悉一下 come 的用法！

1. **come（with）**：用以表示參加說話者或聽話者的動作。

    如：We're going to the party tonight. Would you like to come（with us）?

    （今晚我們要去參加宴會，你要＜跟我們＞來嗎？）

2. **come to**：可表示 reach 或 arrive at 的意思。

    如：Keep straight on until you come to an intersection.

    （直走，直到你到達一個十字路口。）

3. **come from**：用於告訴別人有關某人來自何處。

    如：She comes from England.（她來自英國。）

4. **come on**：用於告訴別人跟隨的意思。

    如：You go first. I'll come on later.（你先走，我隨後就來。）

5. **come out**：表示某物顯現、出現的意思。

    如：(1) The stars came out.（星星出來了。）

    　　(2) When will his new book come out ?

    　　　（他的新書將於何時出版？）

我們接下來看看 come 的用法！

展現英文魅力的尤物：Come動開片語

❖ 從生活中最常用的 come 學習！

☐☐ **come along** 過來；伴隨；陪伴

➻ **Come along！** 來陪伴我！

➻ Why don't you **come along** with us to the party？
你何不陪我們一起去參加宴會呢？

☐☐ **come about** 發生

➻ How did it all **come about**？
這事如何發生的？

☐☐ **come across** 偶然遇到

➻ I **came across** him by chance last Monday.
上禮拜一我偶然地遇見他。

☐☐ **come around** 訪問；再臨

➻ I will **come around** and see you one of these days.
這幾天我會過來拜訪你。

➻ Christmas will soon **come around**.
聖誕節又即將來臨。

☐☐ **come down** 跌落；跌價；生病

➻ He **came down** in the world.
他的社會地位跌落。

➻ The prices will **come down**.
物價會下跌。

➻ The price of the company's stocks will not **come down**.
那家公司的股票價格將不會下跌。

➻ I am **coming down** with something. 我生病了。

展現英文魅力的尤物：Come動詞片語

☐☐ **come by** 獲得；（順路）造訪

　　↦ How did they **come by** all that wealth？
　　　他們如何獲得所有那些財富？

　　↦ Why don't you **come by** some time after ten？
　　　你何不在十點以後來造訪一下？

☐☐ **come in** 進入；開始流行；抵達

　　↦ Please **come in**.
　　　請進。

　　↦ Long dresses have **come in** this year.
　　　今年開始流行長衣。

　　↦ The plane **came in** 30 minutes late.
　　　飛機遲了三十分鐘抵達。

☐☐ **come off** 成功；脫落

　　↦ Will that idea **come off**？
　　　那個主意會成功嗎？

　　↦ Your shirt button is **coming off**！
　　　你衣服的鈕扣掉下來了！

☐☐ **come on** 趕快；予人某種印象

　　↦ **Come on**！趕快！

　　↦ He **comes on** strong.
　　　他看起來很強壯。

☐☐ **come out** 發表；出現

　　↦ New models of Japanese cars usually **come out** in the
　　　spring. 日本新車經常在春季發表。

展現英文魅力的尤物：Come動詞片語

☐☐ **come over** 侵佔；影響；訪問

→ A strange feeling **came over** me.
一股奇怪的感覺盤據了我。

→ When did he **come over** to see you?
他什麼時候來拜訪過你？

☐☐ **come to** 總數達～；發生

→ How much does it all **come to**?
這全部價值多少？

→ What does it all **come to**?
事情到底是怎麼發生的？

☐☐ **come to see you** 拜訪；過來看看

→ When may I **come to see you**?
我什麼時候可以過來看你？

→ I'll **come to see** your place.
我會過來瞧瞧你住的地方。

☐☐ **how come** 為何

→ **How come** you're still working?
你為何仍在工作呢？

☐☐ **come again** 請再說一遍；再來

→ **Come again**? I didn't hear what you said.
請再說一遍，我沒有聽見你的話。

→ May I **come again** some other time?
我可以改天再來嗎？

展現英文魅力的尤物：Come助詞片語

❖ 按字母順序來看看 come 的説法

☐☐ **come across** 偶然遇到；使想起

☐☐ **come along** 趕快；伴隨

☐☐ **come at** 得到；襲擊

☐☐ **come back** 回來；憶起

☐☐ **come face to face with** 與～面對面

☐☐ **come from** 來自～；出生於～

⇨ Where do you come from?
你從什麼地方來的？

☐☐ **come home** 返國；歸鄉；（＋to）深感～

☐☐ **come in** 開始流行；進入；抵達

＊＋contact with 與～有交接；＋sight of 看見

☐☐ **come into** 繼承

＊＋being 出現；＋play 付之使用

☐☐ **come of** 出身；因～而產生

⇨ Poverty often comes of idleness.
貧窮常是懶散的結果。

☐☐ **come off** 舉行；離開；成功；脱落

☐☐ **come on** 趕快 回Hurry up

☐☐ **come out** 出現；發行；結果；（＋of）出自～

⇨ This weekly comes out once a week.
這週刊每週發行一次。

展現英文魅力的尤物：Come 助詞片語

☐☐ **come short of** 缺少

⇨ Come short of change. 缺少零錢。

☐☐ **come to oneself** 恢復知覺

☐☐ **come true** 實現

☐☐ **come up** 接近；發芽

⇨ Christmas is coming up soon. 耶誕節快要到了。

⇨ The seeds I sowed last week haven't come up yet.

我上週種的種子尚未發芽。

☐☐ **come up to** 達到

☐☐ **come up with** 追上～

☐☐ **come upon** 降臨；攻擊；無意中發現

⇨ In reading the Bible, I came upon this verse.

在讀聖經時，我無意中發現這一句。

☆ come to ＋名詞　得到～

⇨ come to hand 到手

☆ come to ＋動詞　到達了明白之點

⇨ How did you come to hear of it ?

你是怎麼聽到這件事的？

☆ come to ＋人　想起；憶及

⇨ It comes to me that I owe you some money.

我想起我欠你一些錢。

6. Go動詞
通往英文殿堂的大道

——前面一章，我們已學到 go 的用法是從某個地方離去，與 come 的方向相反。現在讓我們 " go over " 一下！

複習一下 go 的用法！

1. 與副詞或介詞連接，表示「去」、「離去」的意思。

如：I will not go to such a place. （我才不去那種地方。）

2. 用於現在完成式，表示「死亡」、「消失」的意思。

如：(1) Poor Tom has gone. （可憐的湯姆死了。）

(2) The pain has gone. （疼痛已經消失。）

3. 與副詞或相當副詞的形容詞連用，表示進行的狀態。

如：All has gone well with our plan. （我們的計劃順利進行。）

4. be going to：用以表示未來打算、決定或計劃做某事。

如：I'm going to have my own way. （我要照自己的意思去做。）

5. 用於表示習慣於某種狀態或過慣某種生活。

如：(1) He went in fear of his life. （他經常恐懼會喪失生命。）

(2) She is six months gone. （她已懷孕六個月了。）

go 另外還有一個用法必須注意。我們說「他曾到過中國」，不能用 " He has ***gone*** to China." 而應該是用 " He has ***been*** to China." 因為前者表示「他到中國去了」，可能現在還在中國，或者是往中國的途中。

以下有關 go 的用法，請您來品味！

通往英文殿堂的大道：Go 動詞片語

❖ 從生活最常用的 go 學起！

☐☐ **go ahead** 不猶豫的向前進；做下去

   »→ Go ahead! 前進吧！

☐☐ **go along** 繼續；進行

   »→ You will understand it as you **go along**.
      繼續下去，你就會了解它。

☐☐ **go along with** 陪伴；贊同

   »→ **Go along with** you! 〔俗〕別胡說了！去你的！

   »→ I will **go along with** you as far as the station.
      我會陪你走，一直到車站。

   »→ I see that you're **going along with** a foreigner.
      我看到你跟一個外國人同行。

☐☐ **go back on** 違背（諾言）

   »→ Don't **go back on** your promise.
      不要食言。

☐☐ **go by** 經過；走過

   »→ I'm **going by** the post office.
      我經過郵局。

☐☐ **go for** 去獲得；去取來

   »→ Will you **go for** lost balls?
      你可以把掉了的球撿回來嗎？

☐☐ **go in** 進入

   »→ How shall I **go in**? 我怎麼進去呢？

通往英文殿堂的大道：Go動詞片語

☐☐ **go in for** 喜愛；參加

›→ I think I'll **go in for** tennis.
我想我會去打網球。

›→ He **goes in for** whatever he finds interesting at the moment. 任何東西，在那一剎那能讓他開心，他都喜愛。

☐☐ **go on** 繼續

›→ Do you have enough information to **go on**？
你有足夠的情報來繼續進行下去嗎？

☐☐ **go out** 熄滅

›→ All the lights **went out**！停電了！

☐☐ **go over** 審查；與人～印象

›→ Will you **go over** my plan？
你要看看我的計劃嗎？

›→ The film is **going over** big with audiences.
這部影片深獲觀衆好評。

☐☐ **go through** 完成；通過；售完

›→ I have to **go through** the task by tomorrow.
明日之前我必須完成工作。

›→ The bill **went through** the Congress.
國會通過這項法案。

›→ This book has **gone through** eight editions.
這本書已賣完八版了。

通往英文殿堂的大道：Go 動詞片語

❖ *按字母順序來看 go 的説法*

☐☐ **go a long way** 走一段長路；大有助益

☐☐ **go about** 走來走去；四處走動；著手；做；流傳
　　⇨ Go about your business！ 別管閒事！
　　⇨ The rumor soon went about.
　　　　謠言很快地流傳。

☐☐ **go abroad** 往外國去

☐☐ **go against** 反對

☐☐ **go ahead** 先走；做下去

☐☐ **go along** 進行；陪伴；贊同

☐☐ **go away** 離去；走開

☐☐ **go back on** 違背（諾言等）；背叛

☐☐ **go bad** 變壞；腐敗

☐☐ **go by** 過去；遵循；經過
　　⇨ Two weeks went by. 兩個禮拜過去了。

☐☐ **go down** 沈沒；落下　　圆 go up 昇起
　　⇨ go down on one's knees 跪下

☐☐ **go far** 著名；扯遠了；太過分
　　⇨ You went too far in your joke.
　　　　你的玩笑開得過火了。

☐☐ **go for** 去獲得；去延請
　　⇨ He went for the doctor. 他去請醫生。

通往英文殿堂的大道：Go動詞片語

☐☐ **go home** 回家 　 圆 stay out 不回家

☐☐ **go in** 進入；放入

☐☐ **go in for** 愛好；嗜好；參加

☐☐ **go into** 進入；加入；審查；考慮；討論

☐☐ **go on** 繼續

☐☐ **go out** 離開；熄滅

☐☐ **go out of** 不復；停止

　　　* go out of fashion 不再流行
　　　go out of print 絕版

☐☐ **go over** 查看；複習；背叛；越過；與人～印象

☐☐ **go through** 審閱；忍受；耗盡；通過

☐☐ **go to** 開始做～；等於

　　　⇨ Twelve inches go to one foot.

　　　十二英吋等於一英尺。

☐☐ **go to sleep** 去睡覺

☐☐ **go to sea** 當船員；出海　* go to the sea 到海邊

☐☐ **go to pieces** 破碎；崩潰

☐☐ **go to the bad** 墮落

☐☐ **go to war** 開戰

　　　* go to the war(s) 出征；上戰場

☐☐ **go to school（church）** 上學（教堂）

通往英文殿堂的大道：Go 動詞片語

- [ ] **go to the country** 舉行大選　＊ go into the country 到鄉下
- [ ] **go to work** 去工作
- [ ] **go together** 相配；調和
- [ ] **go under** 沈沒；毀滅
- [ ] **go up** 高漲
  ⇨ Prices are going up every day. 物價每日高漲。
- [ ] **go upon** 破費
- [ ] **go without** 沒有～；自不待言
  ⇨ They go without shoes. 他們沒有穿鞋子。
  ⇨ That goes without saying. 那自不待言。

☆ go with ＋人　陪伴～人；同意～人
　　go with ＋物　配合；附屬於～

☆ go wrong with ＋人　寃枉～人
　　go wrong with ＋物　～故障　囝 go well 狀況良好

♤ Bill goes for Kate.
比爾喜歡凱特。

7.Take動詞
獲取英文資源的利器

　　——有人説，單「take＋名詞」的用法，就占了英語世界的三分之一，這顯示出 take 這個動詞運用的廣泛。take 是指將東西往自己的方向移動，表示「拿到手中」的動作，和 give 正好相反。

溫習一下 take 的用法！

1. 表示「**握**」、「**執**」、「**抱**」的意思：

　　如：She took my hand.（她握住我的手。）

2. 表示「**捕捉**」、「**獲得**」的意思：

　　如：The rabbit was taken in a trap.（那兔子被陷阱捉到了。）

3. 表示「**攜帶**」、「**拿走**」的意思：

　　如：Take her some flowers.（帶一些花給她。）

4. 表示「**享受**」、「**得到**」的意思：

　　如：Let's go into the garden and take some air.

　　　（咱們到花園透透氣。）

5. 表示「**接受**」、「**領受**」的意思：

　　如：Do you take this man to be your husband？

　　　（妳接受此人爲妳丈夫嗎？）

6. 表示「**花費（時間）**」的意思：

　　如：The work took four hours.（這工作花了四個小時。）

take 拿

give 給

獲取英文資源的利器：Take動詞片語

❖ 從生活最常用的 take 動詞學習！

☐☐ **take a taxi** 搭計程車

　　»→ She **takes a taxi** from the station to her house.
　　　　她從車站搭計程車回家。

☐☐ **take a meal** 吃飯

　　»→ They **take** their **meals** at the hotel.
　　　　他們在飯店吃飯。

☐☐ **take a room** 租房間

　　»→ He **took a room** at the Grand Hotel.
　　　　他在圓山大飯店租了一個房間。

☐☐ **take a seat** 坐下；就坐

　　»→ Please **take a seat**. 請坐下。

☐☐ **take a short cut** 走捷徑；抄小路

　　»→ Let's **take a short cut**. 讓我們走捷徑吧！

☆ take＋名詞　去做～；享受～

• take a walk →散步　　　　• take a nap →小睡

• take a trip →旅行　　　　• take a holiday →休假

• take a bath →洗澡　　　　• take a photo →照相

• take a step →踏出一步　　• take a view of →探～的看法

• take a stride upward →向上走

• take an examination →參加考試

• take a fresh start →重新開始

獲取英文資源的利器：Take 助詞片語

☐ **take after** 相似；像

➻ He **takes after** his father.
　他像他父親。

➻ She **takes after** her mother in looks.
　她的長相肖似她的母親。

☐ **take back** 撤銷；取回

➻ I'll **take back** all I said.
　我會取消所有我說過的話。

➻ She **took back** the coat she lent me.
　她取回借給我用的外套。

☐ **take down** 拿下；拆下

➻ **Take down** those curtains and send them to be cleaned.
　拆下這些窗簾，把他們拿去洗。

☐ **take up** 拿起；繼續；消耗

➻ He **took up** his pen and began to write.
　他拿起筆開始寫。

➻ Let's **take up** this matter after lunch.
　午餐後我們再繼續做這件事。

➻ Cooking **takes up** too much time.
　做飯消耗太多時間。

☐ **take A for B** 誤認A為B

➻ She **took** me **for** Mr. Lee.
　她誤認為我是李先生。

獲取英文資源的利器：Take動詞片語

□□ **take in** 收容；收進

»→ The hospital **took** him **in** yesterday.
他昨天住院了。

□□ **take in** 吸引；迷住

»→ She **took** us all **in** with her smile.
我們全被她的微笑所迷住了。

□□ **take in** 看；參觀

»→ In Taipei did you **take in** all the sights？
你參觀台北所有的景觀了嗎？

□□ **take it** 忍受；掛心；悲傷

»→ I'm not going to **take it** any more.
我沒法再忍受了。

»→ Don't **take it** so hard！
不要太悲傷！

□□ **take off** 脫掉

»→ Please **take off** your shoes.
請脫下鞋子。

□□ **take off** 起飛

»→ **Taking off** is easier than landing.
起飛比降落容易。

□□ **take a day off** 休息一天

»→ He **took a day off**. 他休一天假。

獲取英文資源的利器：Ｔａｋｅ動詞片語

☐☐ **take on** 雇用

→ He **took on** extra workers.
他雇用臨時工人。

☐☐ **take on** 接受

→ I **took on** the job at a private school.
我接受私立學校的這份工作。

☐☐ **take place** 發生

→ The accident **took place** on the highway.
車禍發生在公路上。

☐☐ **take time** 需要花時間；騰出時間

→ It **takes time**. 這需要花時間。

→ He studied hard, hardly **taking time** out for lunch.
他很用功，很少挪出時間出去吃午飯。

☐☐ **take up with** 與～相交

→ The man **took it up with** his wife.
這男人和他的太太交往。

☐☐ **take for granted** 視為理所當然

→ He **took** it **for granted** that she was happy.
他認為她快樂是理所當然的事。

☐☐ **take it easy** 休息

→ After working all week, we **took it easy** on Sunday.
經過一週的工作，我們在週日休息。

獲取英文資源的利器：Take 動詞片語

☐☐ take care of 照顧

⟿ **Take care of** yourself!

自己照顧自己！

☐☐ take care 小心；注意

⟿ **Take care**! 當心！

☐☐ take care to do 小心去做～

⟿ **Take care to do** this.

做這個時，小心點。

☐☐ take *one's* temperature 量體溫

⟿ Let's **take your temperature** first.

先讓我們量量你的體溫。

⟿ I **took my temperature**, but it was normal.

我量過自己的體溫，但是卻很正常。

☐☐ take *one's* word 相信～人的話

⟿ I **took your word** for it.

這件事我相信你的話。

Take care to do this!

獲取英文資源的利器：Take動詞片語

◈ 按字母順序來看 take 的説法！

☐ **take a deep breath** 深呼吸

☐ **take a fancy for** 對～喜好

☐ **take a favorable turn** 康復

☐ **take *a person's* breath** 引人注目

☐ **take account of** 考慮
　　囡 take no account of ～ 對～不考慮

☐ **take advantage of** 利用；佔～的便宜

☐ **take advice** 聽納忠告
　　⇨ He took some medical advice. 他聽納醫療的勸告。

☐ **take after** 相似；像

☐ **take a breath** 休息以養神

☐ **take by surprise** 出其不意的出現；使吃驚

☐ **take care of** 照顧

☐ **take a cold** 感冒

☐ **take courage** 需要勇氣
　　⇨ It took courage to go there. 要去那裏需要勇氣。

☐ **take delight in** 樂於；高興

☐ **take effect** 生效
　　⇨ The medicine took effect. 這藥發生效力。

☐ **take fire** 著火；發怒

☐ **take ～ for granted** 視為理所當然

☐ **take heart** 受到鼓勵；振作精神

獲取英文資源的利器：Take 動詞片語

☐☐ **take heart to V** 用心去做

☐☐ **take to heart** 深爲～所感動；對～認眞

☐☐ **take in** 拘捕；收容

☐☐ **take ～ in good part** 善意　囚 **take ～ in ill part** 惡意

☐☐ **take ～ in hand** 拿～在手上；著手做

☐☐ **take（have）interest in** 對～感興趣

　　* be interested in～ 對～感興趣

　　* have an interest in～ 有利害關係的

　　囚 take no interest in 毫無興趣於～

☐☐ **take notice of** 注意到　囚 **take no notice of** 對～絲毫不注意

☐☐ **take off** 除去；啓程；起飛；脫掉

☐☐ **take on** 雇用；接受

☐☐ **take *one's* chance** 碰運氣

☐☐ **take *one's* choice** 選擇

☐☐ **take *one's* own course** （聽其）自然發展

　　⇨ Let things take their own course. 讓事情自然發展。

☐☐ **take *one's* own way** 隨心所欲

☐☐ **take *a person's* part** 偏袒某人

☐☐ **take *a person's* place** 代理～人地位

☐☐ **take *one's* share** 負擔～部分

☐☐ **take *a person's* word** 相信～人的話

☐☐ **take up** 佔據；吸水

　　⇨ A sponge takes up water. 海綿會吸水。

獲取英文資源的利器：Take動詞片語

☐ **take** *one's* **time** 不慌不忙；從容自在

☐ **take pains** 辛苦工作

⇨ He has taken much pain in this work.
在這個工作中，他工作得很辛苦。

☐ **take part in** 參與；參加

☐ **take part with** 與～合作

☐ **take pity on** 因同情而幫助

☐ **take place** 發生；舉行

☐ **take pride in** 以～為榮

☐ **take side** 站在某一方立場

☐ **take trouble** 費心；費力

☐ **take trouble to V** 費（心）力作

* have trouble to do ～ 費心（力）做
* get into trouble 遇上麻煩

☐ **take time** 需要花時間

☐ **take to** 喜歡；耽於；去；用手段

⇨ The dog seldom takes to strangers. 狗不太喜歡陌生人。

☐ **take turns** 輪流

☐ **take up** 拿起；從事；消耗；與～相交；贊同

☆ take hold of ＋物　抓住；掌握

take hold on ＋人　控制

⇨ He took hold of the new ideas. 他掌握新觀念。

8. Get動詞
提昇英文水準的魔術

—— get 是口語中最常用的動詞之一，含有「得到」、「取得」、「買」、「達到」的意思，也常用在「成為～狀態」,「變成～情形或結果」。

溫習一下 get 的用法！

1. **get ＋受詞**，通常意指「接受」、「獲得」、「取得」的意思。

　　如：I've got a telegram.（我收到一封電報。）

2. **get ＋形容詞（或不定詞、分詞、介系詞、介副詞）**表示某種狀況改變或移動。

　　如：(1) Let's get going!（我們快走吧！）

　　　　(2) Get away from me!（離我遠一點！）

3. **get ＋受詞＋形容詞（或不定詞、分詞等）**表示引起變化或移動。

　　如：I'll get the work done in a week.

　　（我會在一週內把工作做完。）

4. **have ＋ got** 表示所有權、關係，或義務。

　　如：Have you really got to go?（你真的必須走了嗎？）

5. **get ＋副詞（或介系詞）**強調所接續的副詞（介系詞）意義。

　　如：He gets *along* well with his boss.（他和他的上司處得很好。）

　　在韋氏字典中，單 get 這一項，就多達一百種以上的意思和用法，所以有人給它一個尊稱，叫 magic verb（魔術動詞）。

　　繼續請看 get 更精采的用法！

get in 上車

get out 下車

get up 起床

提昇英文水準的魔術：Get 動用片語

◈ 靈活運用 get 動詞

☐☐ **get across** 使渡過；使橫越

»→ He **got across** the river. 他渡過這條河。

☐☐ **get away** 離開；脫逃

»→ I hope to **get away** from Taipei for a few days.
我希望離開台北幾天。

☐☐ **get before** 先～而到

»→ I'll **get** there **before** you will.
我會先你而到那裏。

☐☐ **get behind** 落後

»→ During my illness I **got behind** in my school work.
生病期間我的功課落後許多。

☐☐ **get down** 取下

»→ He **got** the book **down** from the shelf.
他從書架上取下那本書。

☐☐ **get in** 進入；進去

»→ I'll **get in**. 我會進去。

☐☐ **get down to**～ 靜下心去～

»→ **Get down to** your work straight away.
靜下心來馬上工作。

☐☐ **get into** 進入；上（車）

»→ I **got into** a taxi outside Tainan Station.
我在台南車站外上了一部計程車。

提昇英文水準的魔術：Get 動詞片語

☐☐ **get on** 進步；進展

　　↦ My son **gets on** very well at school.
　　　　我的兒子在學校進步相當快。

　　↦ He's **getting on** well in his new business.
　　　　他的新事業進展得很順利。

☐☐ **get on the phone** 與某人聯絡（如打電話）

　　↦ You **get on** the phone and call the doctor.
　　　　你去打電話與醫生聯絡。

☐☐ **get on with** 與～和睦相處

　　↦ He **is getting on with** his cousin.
　　　　他和他表弟和睦相處。

　　↦ He is difficult to **get on with**. 他很難相處。

☐☐ **get off** 下車

　　↦ **Get off** at the next stop.
　　　　下一站下車。

　　↦ I **get off** there, too. I'll go near that store myself.
　　　　我也在那裏下車。我會自己走近那商店。

☐☐ **get out of** 走出去

　　↦ I **got out of** that house.
　　　　我走出那間屋子。

☐☐ **get together** 聚首

　　↦ Shall we **get together** at my house tonight？
　　　　今晚到我家聚一聚如何？

提昇英文水準的魔術：Get 動詞片語

☐☐ **get over** 克服；越過；恢復（健康）

　➻ He **got over** that difficulty.
　　他克服了那個困難。

　➻ You can **get over** the handicap soon.
　　你馬上可以越過那障礙。

　➻ It took me ten days to **get over** my cold.
　　過了十天，我的感冒才好。

☐☐ **get through** 完成

　➻ I'll **get through** it.
　　我會完成它。

　➻ I **got through** the work at six o'clock.
　　我六點鐘做完工作。

☐☐ **get up** 起床

　➻ What time do you **get up** every morning?
　　你每天早上幾點起床？

　➻ I **got up** late this morning.
　　今天早上我起得晚。

☐☐ **get down to business** 做事；去工作

　➻ It's time to **get down to business**.
　　是時候了，該工作了。

☐☐ **get ahead** 成功

　➻ You can't **get ahead** if you don't work hard.
　　如果不努力工作，你不會成功的。

提昇英文水準的魔術：Get助開片語

☐ **get at** 意指

→ What are you **getting at**?
　　你意指爲何？

☐ **get back** 回來

→ When did you **get back** from your trip?
　　你旅行何時回來？

☐ **get in touch with** 與～連絡

→ **Get in touch with** me as soon as you arrive here.
　　一到這兒儘快與我連絡。

☐ **get married** 結婚

→ When did she **get married**?
　　她什麼時候結婚的？

☐ **get sick** 生病

→ If you eat too much, you'll **get sick**.
　　吃太多會生病的。

☐ **get hold of** 找到

→ Where can I **get hold of** a good tax lawyer?
　　在那裏可以找到一位好的訴訟律師？

☐ **get rid of** 擺脫糾纏；去掉

→ We finally **got rid of** our old car.
　　我們終於丟掉了我們的老爺車。

提昇英文水準的魔術：Get動開片語

❖ 按字母順序，精通 get 的用法！

☐☐ **get along** 漸暮；（＋with）與人和睦相處；（＋well）成功；繁榮

☐☐ **get at** 意指；了解

☐☐ **get away** 離去；脫逃

☐☐ **get back** 回來　＊ get ＋物＋ back 把物取回

☐☐ **get better** 好轉

☐☐ **get hold of** 找到；得到

⇨ I'll explain, and you'll get hold of the idea.
　　我會解釋，你就會了解這個主意。

☐☐ **get in** 進入；（＋with）與～交往

☐☐ **get off** 下車；脫下

☐☐ **get on** 上車；進步；變老；（＋with）與～相處

⇨ There is no getting on with a suspicious man.
　　與好猜忌的人無法相處。

☐☐ **get out** 下車；洩露秘密；（＋of）逃出

☐☐ **get over** 克服；恢復

☐☐ **get rid of** 除去

☐☐ **get to** 開始；著手

⇨ I got to know Mary at the party.
　　我在宴會中開始認識瑪麗。

☆ get ＋人＋ to V 使人去做～　⇨ I got her to buy us lunch.
　　get ＋物＋過去分詞　物被～　⇨ I get my hair cut.

give 給

take 拿

9. Give動詞

傳授英文溝通的技巧

——大家都知道 give 是「給」的意思。例：I gave David a book.（我給大衛一本書。）但是 give 的意思不僅於此，還有…

溫習一下 give 的用法！

1. 當做及物動詞，有「**交付**」、「**讓與**」、「**產生**」等意思。

　如：(1) Give the porter your bags.（把你的袋子交給搬伕。）

　　　(2) Give me five minutes and I'll change the wheel.

　　　　（給我五分鐘時間來換輪子。）

　　　(3) The sun gives light to us.（太陽給我們光。）

　　＊ give ＋間接受詞＋直接受詞＝ give ＋直接受詞＋ to ＋間接受詞

　　　如：Give me a drink. = Give a drink to me.（給我一杯飲料。）

2. 用於祈使句表示「**偏愛**」或「**選擇**」。

　如：Give me liberty or give me death.（不自由毋寧死。）

3. 當做不及物動詞，有「**讓步**」、「**彎曲、凹下**」等意思。

　如：(1) We mustn't give way to these unreasonable demands.

　　　　　（我們不可對這些不合理要求讓步。）

　　　(2) His knees seemed to give.（他的膝蓋像是直不起來。）

　　在 give 的片語裏面，***give up*** 和 ***give in*** 都具有放棄的意思，但是兩者有區別，前者是對於事物或狀況的放棄，後者則是對於人的投降、放棄。

例：(1) I can do nothing more; I give up.⇒我已無能為力,我放棄了。

　　(2) He has given in to my views.⇒他已接受我的觀點。

接著來學習更多 give 的說法！

傳授英文溝通的技巧：Give 助詞片語

❖ 看最常用的 give，來加強實力！

☐☐ **give and take** 互相遷就

➻ In marriage there should be equal **give and take**.
對婚姻而言夫妻應互相遷就。

☐☐ **give or take** 大約；上下；左右

➻ I weigh 70 kilos, **give or take** a few kilos.
我體重七十公斤左右。

☐☐ **give up** 戒除；放棄；犧牲

➻ I'll **give up** smoking. 我會戒煙的。

➻ Don't **give up** just because it's difficult.
不要因困難而放棄。

➻ She **gave up** everything for her children.
她為孩子犧牲一切。

☐☐ **give in** 投降；屈服

➻ I **give in**. Let's not argue any more.
我們不要再爭論了，我投降了。

☐☐ **give in to** 服從

➻ I have to **give in to** his order.
我必須服從他的命令。

☐☐ **give away** 贈送；洩漏

➻ He **gave away** all his money. 他捐出所有的錢。

➻ Don't **give** the secret **away** to anyone.
不要把秘密洩漏給任何人。

傳授英文溝通的技巧：Give動詞片語

☐ give a talk
☐ give a lecture　演講

　➺ The **lecture** you **gave** yesterday was a masterpiece.
　　你昨天的演講實在是絕妙之作。

☐ give out 分發

　➺ Are you **giving out** meal tickets here?
　　你們這裏分發糧票嗎？

☐ give a ring 打電話

　➺ **Give** me **a ring** if you find out anything.
　　發現任何事情打電話給我。

　➺ I will **give** you **a ring** every night.
　　我每天晚上會打電話給你。

☐ give out 用完；用盡

　➺ After two days our food **gave out**.
　　兩天以後，我們的食物吃光了。

☐ give place to 被～取代

　➺ In the nineteenth century gas light **gave place to** electric light.
　　十九世紀瓦斯燈被電燈所取代。

☐ give the cold shoulder to 冷淡

　➺ After the scandal, his neighbors **gave** him **the cold shoulder**. 醜聞過後，他的鄰居們對他很冷淡。

傳授英文溝通的技巧：Give 的用片語

◆ 按字母順序，來學 give 的用法！

☐ **give attention to** 注意；留意

☐ **give away** 捐贈；洩漏
　　⇨ Don't give away my secret！不要洩漏我的秘密！

☐ **give forth** 發出；公布
　　⇨ The news of his arrival was given forth.
　　　他到達的消息傳出去了。

☐ **give in** 屈服；投降
　　⇨ Don't give in while you're still able.
　　　只要一息尚存，勿投降。

☐ **give oneself to** 專心致力於～；奉獻～
　　⇨ give one's life to～ 將生命奉獻給～

☐ **give out** 分發；發出；用完；公布
　　⇨ The teacher gave out the exam papers. 教師分發試卷。

☐ **give over** 停止；交付；放棄

☐ **give up** 停止；戒除；放棄；投降

☐ **give rise to** 引起

☐ **give vent to** 發洩（怒氣等）
　　⇨ He gave vent to his anger. 他在發洩他的怒氣。

☐ **give way** 撤退；讓路；失去自制力；讓位

☆ give＋人＋a free hand　使～人自由行動
　 give＋人＋a hand　助人一臂之力

10. Put動詞

立下英文不朽的字句

——立法院一向常鬧質詢風波，我們質問別人問題，可以説 ***put*** a question to a person, 而風波的產生，是因為被質詢者 every insult was ***put on*** him. 難怪很多人無法 ***put up with*** it, 而我們這些升斗小民也不禁要對這些人員的素質 ***put*** a question mark（打問號）了。

溫習一下 put 的用法！

1. 當做「**放**」「**置**」，指**處於某種位置**的意思：

　　如：He put the book on the table.（他把書放在桌上。）

2. 使**成為某種狀態或關係**：

　　如：Put yourself in my place.（請替我設身處地想想。）

3. 「**寫下**」，「**記錄**」，「**簽署**」的意思：

　　如：Put your name on this paper.（把你的名字寫在這張紙上。）

4. 當做「**翻譯**」、「**說明**」解：

　　如：(1) Put it into English.（把它翻譯成英文。）

　　　　(2) How shall I put it?（我怎樣說明才好呢？）

5. **使某人承受**（精神或道德的壓力）：

　　如：Don't put all the blame on me.（不要完全歸咎於我。）

　　在片語中，put 的用法就更多了，像 put down 可引申為「消除；制止」的意思。例：put down hecklers at a meeting.（制止會議上詰難的人。）

　　接下來我們來看 put 的用法。

立下英文不朽的字句：Put動開介詞片語

◆ 學習生活最常用的 put !

□□ **put on** 穿上

→ What shall I **put on** over my sweater ?
在毛線衫上，我應該穿上什麼才好？

□□ **put on** 使可利用

→ Would you **put on** the air conditioning ?
開一下冷氣好嗎？

□□ **put on weight** 體重增加

→ I'm **putting on weight** again. 我體重又增加了。

□□ **put off** 延期

→ Don't **put off** till tomorrow what you can do today.
今天能做的就不要延到明天。

→ Can't you **put** it **off** until tomorrow ?
你不能把它延到明天嗎？

□□ **put out** 熄滅

→ Would you **put out** the candles ?
把蠟燭吹熄，好嗎？

□□ **put out** 出版；發行

→ That company **puts out** a magazine, doesn't it ?
那家公司出版了一本雜誌，是嗎？

□□ **put out** 花費；使用

→ I **put out** a lot of money for my son's education.
我為我兒子的教育花了一大筆錢。

立下英文不朽的字句：Put動詞介詞片語

☐ **put up to** 通知

→ Who **put** you **up to** it?
這是誰通知你的？

☐ **put …… up** 住宿；過夜

→ Will you **put** us **up** for one night?
你能讓我們住一晚嗎？

☐ **put up with** 忍受；忍耐

→ If you can **put up with** us, put us up.
如果你受得了我們，就忍受吧。

☐ **put down** 下車；放下

→ I **put** them **down** at Kenting.
在墾丁我讓他們下車。

☐ **put down** 放下

→ Will you **put down** that paper and listen to me?
請你放下報紙，聽我講好嗎？

☐ **put down** 記錄下來

→ Please **put** it **down**. 請記下來。

☐ **put down** 降落

→ The plane **put down** at Taoyuan Airport on time.
這飛機準時降落在桃園機場。

☐ **put in** 花（時間）

→ Let's **put in** a lot of time on that project.
讓我們花多一點時間在那個計劃上。

立下英文不朽的字句：Put 動詞介詞片語

❖ 按字母順序來記憶 put 的説法！

☐☐ **put away** 儲蓄；貯存

☐☐ **put back** 阻礙；阻止　囝 put ahead 前進
⇨ The drivers' strike has put our deliveries back one month. 司機罷工使我們送貨受阻了一個月。

☐☐ **put forth** 長出；發行；發表

☐☐ **put in for** 申請
⇨ She put in for a raise. 她要求加薪。

☐☐ **put off** 延期；推拖；消除
⇨ You must put off your doubts. 你必須消除疑慮。

☐☐ **put on** 穿戴；偽裝；增加；演出；課税

☐☐ **put on an act** 裝模作樣

☐☐ **put out** 逐出；熄滅；使困惑；生產；用力

☐☐ **put through** 接通電話；實現；完成

☐☐ **put up** 升起；建築；提名～候選人；公告；住宿；從事

☐☐ **put upon** 占～便宜
⇨ She felt put upon when asked to work late.
當要求她加班時，她覺得被占了便宜。

☐☐ **put up with** 忍受

☐☐ **put across** 説明白
⇨ She put across her new idea.
她把她的新觀念説明白。

11.Make動詞

製造英文奇蹟的媒人

——看過「屋頂上的提琴手」的人都知道 " match-maker " 這個字是「媒人」的意思，用片語來說是 a person who makes a match，make 此時是「使成為」的意思。另外，也可以解釋為「火柴製造者」，match 從「匹配」變為「火柴」，make 從「成為」變成「製造」，妙不妙？

溫習一下make 的用法！

1. **make ＋受詞＋原形動詞**

   如：I made her cry.（我把她弄哭了。）

2. **make 在被動語態中，要用不定詞**

   如：He was made to go.（他被派前往。）

3. **make 可接兩個受詞**

   如：Can you make me a new suit?（你可以幫我做套新衣服嗎?）

4. **make ＋受詞＋受詞補語**

   如：His father will make him a merchant.

   （他父親會使他成為商人。）

5. 當做「**估計**」的意思：

   如：What do you make of the time?（你認為現在幾點鐘？）

6. 當做「**得到**」的意思：

   如：He made a fortune on the Stock Exchange.

   （他買賣股票發了財。）

   繼續來看看make 的其他用法！

製造英文奇蹟的媒人：Make動詞片語

◆ 靈活運用 make 的慣用句！

☐☐ **make it** 達成預定目標；趕上；成功

　　↣ Can you **make it** on time？
　　　你能在預定時間完成嗎？

　　↣ I barely **made** the 9:20 train.
　　　我幾乎無法趕上九點二十分的火車。

　　↣ I bet he won't **make it**. 我打賭他不會成功。

☐☐ **make for** 去向

　　↣ Where were you **making for** last night？
　　　你昨晚跑到哪裏了？

☐☐ **make out** 了解

　　↣ I can't **make out** what you are saying.
　　　我無法了解你所說的。

☐☐ **make out** 成功；進展

　　↣ He **made out** really well in the clothing business.
　　　他在服飾業相當成功。

　　↣ How are you **making out**？ 你的進展如何？

☐☐ **make sense** 合情合理

　　↣ He **makes sense**.
　　　他說得很合理。

　　↣ This **makes no sense**. 這不合理。

　　＊ make sense 的相對詞是 make no sense, don't make any sense。

製造英文奇蹟的媒人：Make動詞片語

☐☐ make up 和解；復交

»→ They **made up** and became friends again.
他們言歸於好，再度成為朋友。

☐☐ make up 占據

»→ Advertising **makes up** about 7% of this company's
expenses. 廣告占了這家公司經費的百分之七。

☐☐ make up of 組成

»→ Water is **made up of** hydrogen and oxygen.
水是由氫和氧組成。

»→ The earth is **made up of** sea and land.
地球是由水和陸地組成。

☐☐ make up for 補償；賠償

»→ I will **make up for** it next time. 下次我會補償的。

»→ You must **make up for** the loss. 你必須賠償損失。

☐☐ make up one's mind 下定決心

»→ I've **made up my mind**.
我已經下定決心。

»→ I wish he would **make up his mind** one way or the
other. 我希望他能夠下一個決定。

☐☐ make a hit 受歡迎（喜愛）

»→ Our showroom **made a hit** with young ladies.
我們的貨品陳列室相當受少女的喜愛。

製造英文奇蹟的媒人：Make助動片語

❖ 按字母順序總覽 make 的用法！

☐☐ **make a fool of** 愚弄
　　⇨ Don't make a fool of me. 不要愚弄我。

☐☐ **make a name for** *oneself* 成名

☐☐ **make a fortune** 致富

☐☐ **make away with** 用完；殺死；偷　回 get rid of

☐☐ **make believe** 假裝

☐☐ **make for** 移向；攻擊；促進
　　⇨ The watchdog made for the robber.
　　　看門犬攻擊強盜。

☐☐ **make good** 成功；賠償；實現
　　⇨ He made good on his promise. 他實現諾言。

☐☐ **make out** 完成；了解；成功；分辨

☐☐ **make over** 修改；移交
　　⇨ to make over a dress. 修改衣服。

☐☐ **make sure** 確信；弄清楚

☐☐ **make up** 組成；和解；完成；補償

☆ make A（out）of B　由 B 製成 A
　　Books are made of paper. 書是由紙做的。
☆ A 的本質未變，用 make A of B
　　Wine is made from grapes. 酒是由葡萄釀成的。
☆ A 本質改變的製品，用 make A from B

12. Let動詞
超脫英文侷限的錦囊

—— 美國有一部電影叫做「凡夫俗子」，劇中有句台詞說："Let yourself off the hook." ——hook 就是掛鉤，就像魚，一旦上鉤就成為人們的美食佳餚，因此本句話的意思是指脫離困境。

溫習一下 let 的用法！

1. **let ＋名詞（代名詞）**，表示許可、讓～

   如：Will you let me smoke？（我可以抽煙嗎？）

2. **let ＋第一人稱代名詞（第三人稱代名詞）**，形成間接祈使句

   如：Let's start at once, shall we？（我們即刻動身，好嗎？）

3. **let 用在間接祈使句中**可表示假設的意思

   如：Let them all come！（讓他們都來吧！＜我不相信他們都敢來。＞）

4. **let ＋名詞＋原形不定詞＝ let ＋原形不定詞＋名詞**

   如：Let the waitress go.（讓這女侍走。）

   　　＝Let go of the waitress.

5. **let ＋受詞＋受詞補語（形容詞、副詞、介系詞）**，表 let 的結果、狀態。

   如：(1) Let me out！（讓我出去！）

   　　(2) Let me alone！（不要管我！）

   　　(3) Please let me in.（請讓我進去。）

記住 let 是指從某種束縛狀態中「解放」「鬆弛」的意思。如 let down 是放下的意思；let go 是鬆手；let out 是使流出，因此意思較容易掌握。

最後讓我們來學習 let 的用法！

超脫英文侷限的錦囊：Let的相關片語

◆ 從生活中最常用的 let 著手學習！

☐☐ **let alone** 別干涉；別打擾

➺ Don't whisper, **let alone** speak.
　　不要竊竊私語，打擾談話。

➺ I don't want to see him, **let alone** go out with him.
　　我不要見他，叫他別來打擾。

☐☐ **let go** 放手；放開

➺ **Let me go** !
　　讓我走！放開你的手！不要拉我！

☐☐ **let go of** 放開；鬆手

➺ **Let go of** my arm！放開我的手！

➺ As soon as I **let go of** the leash, the dog ran away.
　　我一放開狗鍊，狗馬上跑走。

☐☐ **let down** 使失望

➺ Don't **let** me **down**. 不要讓我失望。

☐☐ **let in** 容許進入；透露秘密

➺ Please **let** me **in**.
　　請允許我進去。

➺ Did they **let in** on the secret？
　　他們透露這個秘密嗎？

☐☐ **let's see if** 查看究竟

➺ **Let's see if** our cars have enough gas.
　　讓我們查看一下我們的車子是否有足夠的汽油。

超脫英文侷限的錦囊：Let的即片語

☐☐ **let up** 停止（指下雨）

»→ The rain never **let up** all night.

　　昨晚的雨下個不停。

»→ I may go out if the rain **lets up**.

　　如果雨停了，我就可以出去了。

☐☐ **let me get** 讓我做～

»→ **Let me get** you something to drink.

　　讓我拿點喝的給你。

»→ **Let me get** you a ticket to the concert.

　　讓我幫你買一張到音樂會的票。

☐☐ **let me help** 讓我幫忙～

»→ **Let me help** you wipe it off.

　　讓我幫你把它擦掉。

»→ **Let me help** you put on your coat.

　　讓我替你穿上外套。

☐☐ **let me take a look** 讓我看一下

»→ **Let me take a look** at your driver's license.

　　讓我看一下你的駕駛執照。

☐☐ **let at it** 讓～做

»→ Don't stop him. **Let** him **at it**.

　　不要阻止他，讓他做。

»→ Will you **let** me **at it**?

　　你會讓我做嗎？

超脫英文侷限的錦囊：Let動用片語

❖ **按字母順序來看看 let 的秘密！**

☐☐ **let alone** 別干涉；別打擾

☐☐ **let be what it may** 不管
  ⇨ Let it be ever so humble, home is home.
    不管再怎麼簡陋，家到底是家。

☐☐ **let go** 放手；革職；無拘束
  ＊ let oneself go 儘情發洩情感、慾望、衝動等

☐☐ **let go of** 手放開

☐☐ **let in** 進入

☐☐ **let into** 嵌入；鑲；告知秘密

☐☐ **let it be done** 就這麼辦

☐☐ **let off** 放（槍、砲）
  ⇨ We let off fireworks. 我們施放煙火。

☐☐ **let on** 洩露（秘密）；假裝
  ⇨ He let on that he didn't see me.
    他假裝沒看到我。

☐☐ **let out at ～** 動手打～；向～猛擊

☆ let ＋目的語＋原形動詞　讓（叫）～做～
  ⇨ let me come（＝Take me）with you. 讓我和你一起走。
  ⇨ Let me go（＝Send me）there. 送我到那裏去。
  ⇨ Let me hear（＝Tell me）the story. 告訴我這個故事。

PART 5

介詞情侶記憶法

白馬王子和白雪公主的結果是？！

●**介詞情侶記憶法的內容**── 針對英文中最出風頭的配
　　　　　　　　　　　　　角─介系詞，詳析4組介
　　　　　　　　　　　　　系詞片語的正反義用法。

　　　特色── 採比較分析法，深入4組
　　　　　　　相反意思的介詞片語中，
　　　　　　　全面融會貫通。

　　　目的── 兩個兩個介詞一起背，節
　　　　　　　省時間，效果宏大。

　　　要訣── 依其意義，對照使用，一
　　　　　　　次記一組，運用在生活當
　　　　　　　中。

1.On & Off 介詞

英文第一對情人的秘密

表接觸的 on，表切斷的 off

英文表示開關方面有兩個字——on 跟 off。On 是表示接入電源，off 則表示切掉。

On 這個字彙是表示接觸、接近、向某位置運動、移動。（請看圖 1）一般表示「在～之上」、「不分開」、「繼續」的意思。Off 是和 on 相反的字彙，表示「從～分開（脫離）」、「切斷、中止」的意思。（請看圖 2）因此基本上，on 和 off 是意思相反的一組介系詞。

除上所述，on 還表示特定的早上、下午、晚上等等時刻。（例：I was born *on* the 31th of May in 1965. ＝我在 1965 年的 5 月 31 日出生。）On 也用在表示狀態、活動，（例：What time are you going *on* duty？＝你什麼時候開始上班？）也用在表示支撐物體。（例：The baby was crawling *on* all fours. ＝嬰孩用四肢爬行。）

Off 則有多種用法，可當介系詞、副詞、形容詞、感嘆詞等等。例如 Sales have been *off* this month. （這個月生意清淡。）這是形容詞的用法。He took a week *off*. （她休假一個禮拜。）是副詞用法。I'm *off* cigarettes for good. （我永遠戒煙。）則是介系詞的用法。

Off 也表示降低價錢，如 Won't you take something *off* this price？（你不能算便宜一點嗎？）

　　我們常把 off 弄錯。這個字主要是表示運動的動詞，用在從某物離開、遷移，或表示有某距離的場合上。看看以下三個句子，很少有學生能弄清楚的。

1. He was off work.
2. He was out of work.
3. He rested from his work.

　　　　　　　　① 他下班了。

　　　　　　　　② 他失業了。

　　　　　　　　③ 他退休了。

　　On 和 off 一起使用的話，有 raining *on and off*（雨一會兒下，一會兒停），I watch TV *off and on*.（我偶爾看電視。）

溫習一下 on 的用法！

1. 表示時間

　　例：We have no class on Sunday.（我們星期天沒課。）

2.「由於～；因爲～」

　　例：I came late on account of the car accident.

　　　　（我因車禍來遲了。）

3.「依靠；賴～爲生」

　　例：The baby was crawling on all fours.（寶寶用四肢爬行。）

4. 表示「在～的狀態或情況中」

　　例：What time are you on duty?（你何時值班？）

5. 作「關於；論及」解

　　例：He has written a book on democracy.

　　　　（他寫了一本有關民主主義的書。）

6. 表示「**方向；朝～**」之意

　例：A pretty girl smiles at him.

　（有個漂亮的小姐朝他微笑。）

溫習一下 off 的用法！

1. 作「**休息**」解

　例：He was off for the afternoon.（他下午休息。）

2. 表示「**離開；中斷**」

　例：(1) The child fell off the tree.（那小孩從樹上摔下來。）

　　　(2) I'm off cigarettes.（我在戒煙。）

3. 表示「**離～有一段距離**」

　例：We are far off the town.（我們遠離市鎮。）

4. 作「**價錢低於～**」解

　例：The sale is 30％ off the original price.

　　　（七折大特賣。）

　　另外，**off and on** 是「**斷斷續續**」的意思，你也可以倒過來說 on and off，意思都是一樣的。看看例句，您便可輕鬆明白：

例：(1) I watch TV off and on.

　　　（我斷斷續續地看電視。）

　　　(2) It rains on and off.（雨斷斷續續地下著。）

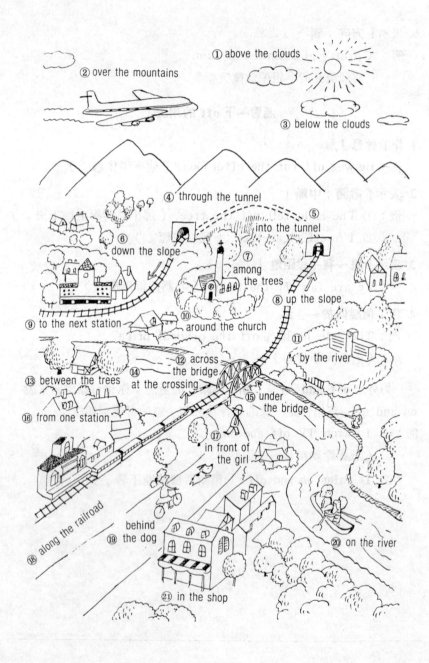

① above the clouds
② over the mountains
③ below the clouds
④ through the tunnel
⑤ into the tunnel
⑥ down the slope
⑦ among the trees
⑧ up the slope
⑨ to the next station
⑩ around the church
⑪ by the river
⑫ across the bridge
⑬ between the trees
⑭ at the crossing
⑮ under the bridge
⑯ from one station
⑰ in front of the girl
⑱ along the railroad
⑲ behind the dog
⑳ on the river
㉑ in the shop

圖解英文介系詞用法

① □□ above the clouds 在雲端之上
② □□ over the mountains 飛越羣山
③ □□ below the clouds 在雲端之下
④ □□ through the tunnel 穿過隧道
⑤ □□ into the tunnel 進入隧道
⑥ □□ down the slope 下坡
⑦ □□ among the trees 在樹林之中
⑧ □□ up the slope 上坡
⑨ □□ to the next station 到下一車站
⑩ □□ around the church 在教堂四週

⑪ □□ by the river 河畔
⑫ □□ across the bridge 越過橋
⑬ □□ between the trees 在兩樹之間
⑭ □□ at the crossing 在鐵路交叉口
⑮ □□ under the bridge 在橋下
⑯ □□ from one station 從一個車站
⑰ □□ in front of the girl 在女孩的前面
⑱ □□ along the railroad 沿著鐵路
⑲ □□ behind the dog 在狗的後面
⑳ □□ on the river 在河上
㉑ □□ in the shop 在商店裏

英文第一對情人的秘密：On 介開片語

◆從生活最常用的 on 片語開始

☐☐ **on account of** 因為
　　➻ I was absent last Tuesday **on account of** illness.
　　　因為生病所以我上週二缺席。

☐☐ **on business** 因商務；因公
　　➻ He went to Tainan **on business.**
　　　他因公到台南。

☐☐ **on demand** 來取即付
　　➻ We'll pay you **on demand** any day after July 10th.
　　　自七月十日以後的任一天，你來取我們馬上付給你。

☐☐ **on duty** 執行勤務
　　➻ He goes **on duty** at 9 a.m. and comes off duty at 6
　　　p.m. 他上午九點開始執勤直到下午六點。

☐☐ **on purpose** 故意的
　　➻ I did it **on purpose.** 我是故意這麼做的。

☐☐ **on sale** 拍賣中
　　➻ The house is **on sale.** 這房子在拍賣中。

☐☐ **on the contrary** 相反地
　　➻ **On the contrary** she said nothing.
　　　相反地，她什麼都沒說。

☐☐ **on the level** 誠實的；直率的
　　➻ Are you **on the level**, David？
　　　大衛，你是真誠的嗎？

英文第一對情人的秘密：On 介詞片語

❖ 按字母順序來看 on 的說法！

☐ **on an average** 平均

☐ **on and on** 一直不斷的

☐ **on behalf of** 爲了（某人利益）；作～之代表

☐ **on duty** 執勤中

☐ **on earth** 究竟；到底；在地球上

☐ **on end** 豎起；連續的

☐ **on fire** 著火了

☐ **on foot** 步行
　　⇨ It takes about half an hour on foot, or ten minutes by car.
　　　徒步約半小時，坐車約十分鐘。

☐ **on good terms with** 與某人友善
　　囚 on bad terms 與某人交惡

☐ **on hand** 持有；蒞臨

☐ **on purpose** 故意的　　＊ to the purpose 得要領；切題

☐ **on sale** 拍賣中；廉價出售　　＊ for sale 出售

☐ **on Sunday** 在星期天
　　＊ on a Sunday 在一個星期天
　　　on Sundays 每個星期天
　　　on Sunday last 上個星期天
　　　on Sunday next 下個星期天

☐ **on the contrary** 相反的　　＊ to the contrary 有相反的情形

英文第一對情人的秘密：On 介詞片語

☐☐ **on the ground** 在地上

☐☐ **on the ground of** 基於～理由

☐☐ **on the heels of** 緊接～之後

☐☐ **on time** 準時
⇨ Be here tomorrow on time. 明天準時到這裏。

☐☐ **on the morning** 某個特定的早晨
＊ in the morning 早晨；this morning 今朝；yesterday morning 昨晨

☐☐ **on the look out for** 警戒

☐☐ **on the one hand ～ and（but）on the other hand**
一方面～，另一方面～

☐☐ **on the other hand** 另一方面

☐☐ **on the part of** 代表某方；在某方面

☐☐ **on the point of** 瀕臨～；正要～
⇨ The train was just on the point of starting when I got to the station.
當我到達火車站時，火車正要開走。
＊ at the point of ～就要～

☐☐ **on the quiet** 秘密的；暗地裏
＊ in the quiet 安靜的；at the quiet 平靜的
· He lives in quiet. 他過著安靜的生活。

☐☐ **on the whole** 整個看起來；大致上
⇨ On the whole, business has improved since last year.
大致上，自去年商務已改善了。

英文第一對情人的秘密：On 介詞片語

☐ **on the side** 本行之外的，為副業〔兼職〕

⇨ make money on the side 兼職賺錢

⇨ There are two ways to make money on the side, he said.
他說以兼職來賺錢有兩種方法。

☐ **on the side of** 站在某一方；偏袒

⇨ Whose side are you on? 你到底站在那一邊的？

⇨ Success is always on the side of the persevering.
成功總是站在堅毅者一方。

☐ **on the spot** 在現場；立刻

⇨ The goods will be sold on the spot. 貨品將被現場拍賣。

⇨ He understands everything right on the spot.
他即刻了解每件事情。

 * at the spot 在～地點　・We met at the spot. 我們在那地點會面。

☐ **on the way** 途中

☐ **on** *one's* **way to** 在某人往～的途中

☐ **on the whole** 全盤而論；大體來講　 * the fact is 事實上

☐ **depend on** 依賴

⇨ Taiwan depends on foreign trade.
台灣依賴外貿為生。

☐ **live on** 賴以為生；靠～過活

⇨ We cannot live on ten thousand NT. dollars a month.
靠每月新台幣一萬元過活，我們實在活不下去。

☐ **cut back on** 縮減

英文第一對情人的秘密：◎off介副片語

◆ 看看生活最常用的 off 片語！

☐ off and on 偶爾；斷斷續續

→ He attends meetings **off and on**.

他偶爾去開會。

→ It has been raining **off and on**.

雨斷斷續續地下著。

☐ off duty 不值勤；不當班

→ I am **off duty** today. 我今天不值班。

→ I'll be **off duty** at noon on Saturday.

星期六中午我就下班了。

☐ off hand 馬上；即席

→ **Off hand**, I'd say her problem is shyness.

我敢立刻斷言，她的問題出在害羞上。

→ He made a splendid speech **off hand**.

他作了一場精采的即席演講。

☐ off with you 拿去；除去

→ Oh, **off with you**. 噢！走開！

☐ off *one's* guard 不警覺；不注意

→ I realize I was **off my guard**.

我了解我太粗心大意。

☐ well off 境況很好

She must be **well off**. 她必定是境況很好。

英文第一對情人的秘密：off 介詞片語

☐☐ call off 取消

→ We have to **call off** the meeting.
我們必須取消會議。

☐☐ cut off 切斷；停止

→ The water has been **cut off**. 停水了。

☐☐ lay off 解雇；休息；戒除

→ They were **laid off** from work. 他們被解僱了。

☐☐ lead off 率先

→ Who's going to **lead off**?
由誰率先開始？

☐☐ pay off 全部清還

→ It took them six years to **pay off**.
他們花了六年才還清債務。

☐☐ play off 加賽一場決定勝負

→ The championship was decided by **playing off** the tie.
平手雙方加賽一場決定冠亞軍。

☐☐ show off 誇耀；炫耀

→ The parade was designed to **show off** all the latest weapons.
這次閱兵是為了炫耀最新武器而舉行的。

→ She enjoys **showing off** her expensive clothes.
她喜愛炫耀她昂貴的衣服。

2. Over & Under 介詞
英文第二對佳偶的結合

Over 是蓋在上面，under 是被蓋在下面

我們常會把 over 和 on 搞混，或把用法弄錯。Over 是表示「離開物品，在其上」的意思，如圖 1，也就是表示「在有某距離的上方」。所以，也表示「在～以上」、「覆蓋於～之上」的動作意思。也被轉用成「越過」、「終了」的意思。

現在先來看看例句，抓住語感：

1. The helicopter hovered over the building.
   直升機在那棟建築物的上面盤旋。

2. The view was splendid over the plain.
   平原之上的景色極佳。

3. This dress cost me over 4,000 NT dollars.
   這件衣服花了我超過台幣四千元。

Over 也和情緒（emotion）、感情（feeling）等動詞連用，表示關心（concern）的意思。用在時間上，是表示某段期間的全部（例：*over the weekend* ＝週末期間）。以上是 over 的主要用法，還有一種用法是 over 和其他字彙的合成語。例如：

· overhead〔′ovɚ,hɛd〕*adj.*,*adv.* 在空中；在上

· overdo〔′ovɚ′du〕*v.* 過分；過火

· overweight〔′ovɚ′wet〕*v.*,*adj.* 超重；過重的

- oversleep〔'ovɚ'slip〕*v*. 睡過頭
- overall〔'ovɚ,ɔl〕*adj*. 全面的；所有的
- overhear〔,ovɚ'hɪr〕*v*. 無意聽到；從旁聽到
- overseas〔'ovɚ'siz〕*adj*. 海外的；國外的
- overfree〔'ovɚ'fri〕*adj*. 太自由的

　　和 over 相反的是 under。Under 是「在～之下」、「被蓋在～之下」的意思。和 over 相比較，還表示在支配、監督等狀況之下。例如 "***under the sun***"，是從「在太陽之下」轉換成「在世界之中」的意思。

* No country ***under the sun*** is safe in this nuclear age.
　　在這個核子的時代裏，世界任何國家都不安全。

　　當然，和 over 一樣，under 也有許多合成語。例如：
- underline〔,ʌndɚ'laɪn〕*v*. 劃線於…之下；加強
- underwear〔'ʌndɚ,wɛr〕*n*. 內衣褲
- undercooked〔,ʌndɚ'kʊkt〕*adj*. 半生不熟的
- undergo〔,ʌndɚ'go〕*v*. 遭受；經歷；忍受
- understatement〔'ʌndɚ,stetmənt〕*n*. 輕描淡寫
- underweight〔'ʌndɚ,wet〕*adj*. 重量不足的

溫習一下 over 的用法！

1. 表示「**在～之上；掩蓋～之上**」
　　例：The helicopter hovered over the building.
　　　　（直昇機掠過建築物上方。）

2. 表示「**遍及～**」
　　例：Rumors were all over the town.（城裏謠言漫天。）

3. 表示「**越過；橫過**」

例：Birds fly over the hill. （鳥飛過山丘。）

4. 表示「**職位高於～；權力大於～**」

例：A general is over a colonel. （將軍階級高於上校。）

5. 表示「**回過頭來**」

例：She stared at me over her shoulder. （她回過頭瞪我。）

6. 表示「**超過某一時間、數量。**」

例：Could you stay here over Sunday ?

（你能待在這裏，過了星期天再走嗎？）

7. 表示「**關於～；一邊～一邊～**」

例：(1) She cried over his death. （她爲他的死而哭。）

(2) We talked over a cup of coffee.

（我們一邊聊天，一邊喝咖啡。）

8. 「**再、又**」「**重複**」之意

例：We have already read it ten times over.

（我們已經連續讀了十遍。）

溫習一下 under 的用法！

1. 表示「**在～之下**」

例：He is swimming under the bridge. （他在橋下游泳。）

2. 表示「**包含於～之中**」

例：Her hair is under her hat. （她的頭髮包在帽子中。）

3. 表示「**在階級或地位上低於～**」「**未滿～**」

例：John is an officer under the rank of colonel.

（約翰是一位上校以下的軍官。）

4. 表示「**在～的監督、統治、指揮、保護之下**」

　　例：The boy is under my charge.（這男孩由我照顧。）

5. 表示「**歸類於～項目**」

　　例：The book is listed under geography.
　　（這本書列入地理學類別下。）

6. 表示「**根據；假借**」

　　例：The star singer was known under a new name.
　　（這位名歌星以新名字為人所知。）

　　Over 和 Under 這對情侶都有一個共同的特性，就是能夠自由自在地與許多不同的字結合，（生性都非常開放！）如 overbuy, overflow, overdo, underline, underwear 等等，實在可以說是「物以類聚」。

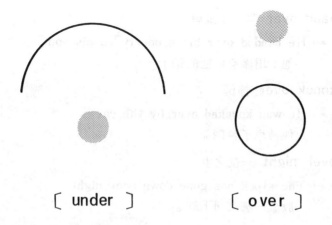

〔 under 〕　　　　〔 over 〕

英文第二對佳偶的結合：Over 介詞片語

◆ 從生活最常用的 over 來品味！

☐ **over again** 再一次

➻ She explained it **over again**.
她再一次解說。

➻ I'd better write **over** this manuscript **again**.
我最好重新謄過一遍這份草稿。

➻ **Over again**？
又要來一次？

☐ **over and over again** 重覆地；再三地

➻ He is writing the manuscript **over and over again**.
他反覆地寫草稿。

☐ **come over** 過來

➻ Can you **come over** here？
你能過來這裏一下嗎？

☐ **hand over** 移交；讓與

➻ He **handed over** his property to his son.
他把財產交給他的兒子。

☐ **knock over** 撞倒

➻ He was **knocked over** by the car.
他被車子撞倒。

☐ **over night** 一夜之中

➻ The stock has gone down **over night**.
股票一夜之間下跌。

英文第二對佳偶的結合：Over 介詞片語

□□ **look over** 回頭看；過目一遍

　　➟ I **looked over** my shoulder.
　　　我轉回頭看。

　　➟ I'll **look over** it after I come back.
　　　回來後，我會細看一遍。

□□ **talk over** 討論

　　➟ Anyway, we'll **talk** it **over** tomorrow.
　　　不管怎樣，我們明天再討論吧。

□□ **over the weekend** 渡週末

　　➟ What are you going to do **over the weekend**?
　　　你打算怎麼渡週末？

□□ **all over** 結束；到處

　　➟ The examinations are **all over**.
　　　考試全部結束。

　　➟ I sweat **all over**.
　　　我渾身是汗。

□□ **over and above** 除了～之外

　　➟ The waiters get good tips **over and above** their wages.
　　　服務生除了薪水以外還可拿到不少的小費。

□□ **cry over** 慟哭

　　➟ Don't cry over spilt milk.
　　　覆水難收。

英文第二對佳偶的結合：Under 介詞片語

❖ under 有以下幾種較常用的片語，請看！

☐ **under age** 未成年

　　⟶ She is still **under age**.
　　　她尚未成年。

☐ **under** *one's* **eyes**（**nose**） 在～眼前；目睹

　　⟶ This happened **under my nose**.
　　　我目睹這件事情發生。

☐ **under** *one's* **belt** 在胃中

　　⟶ John is talkative when he has a few drinks **under his belt**. 約翰幾杯酒下肚後便話多。

☐ **under** *one's* **breath** 小聲的

　　⟶ I told Lucy the news **under my breath**.
　　　我小聲把那消息告訴露西。

☐ **under the counter** 秘密的（買或賣）

　　⟶ That book has been banned, but you can get it there **under the counter**.
　　　那本書已被禁售，但在那裏你可以暗中買到。

☐ **under the head of** 歸～項目之下

　　⟶ Homer's Iliad comes **under the head of** epic poetry.
　　　荷馬的「伊利亞德」屬於史詩類。

☐ **under the weather** 生病

　　⟶ She has been **under the weather** since last Sunday.
　　　她自上星期天就生病了。

英文第二對佳偶的結合：Over & Under 介間片語

◆ 看看 over & under 的其他説法！

☐☐ **over again** 再一次

☐☐ **over and over**（**again**）再三；反覆地

☐☐ **over the sea** 渡海

☐☐ **over there** 在那邊

☐☐ **over here** 在這裏

☐☐ **over** *one's* **head** 超過某人的理解力

⇨ What he said was over my head.
他所說的不是我所能理解的。

☐☐ **under** ＋（**抽象**）**名詞** 在～之中

＊ under construction 建築中　　under medical treatment 治療中
＊ under consideration 考慮中　　under examination 試驗中

⇨ The house is now under construction.
房子正在建築中。

⇨ He's been under treatment. 他正在療養中。

☐☐ **under** *one's* **breath** 小聲的；低聲的

☐☐ **under** *one's* **eyes**（**nose**）在～眼前

☐☐ **under repair** 修理中

⇨ The house is under repair. 房子正在翻修。

＊ in good repair 修理狀況良好

☐☐ **under the sun** 世界上；天下

⇨ The president's assassination shocked everyone under
the sun. 總統遇刺，舉世震驚。

☐☐ **under the weather** 生病的；微有酒意的

3. Up & Down 介詞
英文第三對怨偶的背離

表示向下的 down，表示向上的 up

話，有積極和消極之分。大部分的人是依據心情或節日、事件等來使用 active 或 passive 的話，像 up 就是指充滿信心的、興高采烈的詞語，而 down 既是其相反詞，當然也就是沮喪的、意志消沈的意思了。

1. He was **up** for a time and then, without warning, despondent again.

   他一度興高采烈，但忽然又情緒低沉下來。

2. She felt **down** about his failure.

   她因失敗而覺得沮喪。

Down 是指從上向下移動，或表示在下的靜止狀態。（圖 1 ）本來 down 是由 off the hill （下山丘）的意思而來的。因此，現今的字典中 downs 可當名詞，有山丘的意思。

然而，down 本來的意思不怎麼好，像：

1. Down with the money. （拿出錢來！）

2. Down with the Cabinet （Government）!

   打倒內閣（政府）！

都是不太好的意思，但也有不具任何意義的用法，如：

1. What were you doing down there?

   你在那裏做什麼？

2. Go down the street for about five minutes, and you will see the Department Store to the right.

　　往前走大約五分鐘，向右你就可以看見百貨公司。

　　Go down（up）the street 不一定是指坡道，從這邊（自己的方向）來，是用 up，往正方直去是用 down。但是，up and down the street 則是表示「街上各處」之意。

　　Up 本來的意思是向上提升、運動，表示其最終的位置。（圖 2 ）Up 另外還有許多意思，例如，在地圖上，up 是指北方，往南，則叫做 down。在美國，往商業區走，叫做 down，往住宅區去，則爲 up。上行列車、物價上漲，完成、結束也都是用 up。up 和 down 是屬於積極、好的意思方面的字彙。

　　例如：

1. Our plan is made. Now let's talk it up.

　　計劃已經完成，讓我們宣傳一下吧。

2. Korea is now up and coming. 韓國現正欣欣向榮。

3. Is anything up? 有什麼事嗎？

4. Be up early tomorrow morning. 明早要早起。

　　Up 還有許多很方便的用法，充斥在各類英文句子中，想要精通英語，就必須先通曉此類用法。

複習一下 down 的用法！

1. 表示動作向下，作「**向下**」解

例：The boy ran down the stairs.（那小孩跑下樓梯。）

2. 表示（**趨勢、程度**）衰退；減退

例：The typhoon has gone down.（颱風威力減退。）

3. 表示「**直到～**」

例：Down to date, the story is still popular.

（直到今天，這故事仍受歡迎。）

4. 表示「**沿著～；在～的下游**」

例：(1) I walked down the road.（我沿著這條路走下去。）

(2) The ship sailed down the river.（船順流而行。）

5. 表示「**倒下**」

例：He was knocked down by a car.（他被車撞倒了。）

6. 表示「**自…至～**」

例：The Bill was sent down to the House of Commons.

（該項議案送往下議院。）

7. 表示「（**價格**）**下跌；降低**」

例：(1) The price of rice is down.（稻米價格下跌。）

(2) The temperature went down.（氣溫下降。）

溫習一下 up 的用法！

1. 表示動作向上，作「**向上**」解。

例：The boy ran up the stairs.（那小孩跑上階梯。）

2. 表示「**在上面，升起**」

例：(1) The kite is high up in the sky.（風箏高高在天空。）

　　(2) Is the flag up?（旗升上去了嗎？）

3. 表示「**（價格）上漲；發起**」

例：(1) Prices have gone up.（物價上漲。）

　　(2) My mother's temper is up.（我媽媽發脾氣了。）

4. 表示「**完畢；完結**」

例：Time is up.（時間到了。）

5. 表示「**發生**」

例：What is up there?（那邊發生什麼事了？）

6. 表示「**沿著**」

例：We walked up the street.（我們沿著街道走。）

7. 表示「**在～的上游**」

例：The village is up the river.（這村莊在河的上游。）

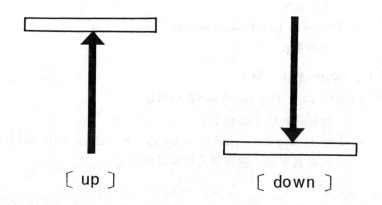

〔 up 〕　　　　　〔 down 〕

英文第三對怨偶的背離：Up & Down 介詞片語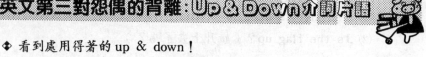

❖ 看到處用得著的 up & down！

☐☐ **up and down** 到處；來來去去

↦ I have looked for it **up and down**.
我已四處在搜尋。

↦ We walked **up and down** the streets of Taipei.
我們在台北街頭四處走。

↦ He walked **up and down** the room.
他在房間裏來回踱步。

☐☐ **down with** 倒下；躺在床上

↦ I have been **down with** a cold.
我感冒躺在床上。

↦ I have been **down with** a headache.
我頭痛躺在床上。

☐☐ **break down** 故障；失敗

↦ The car **broke down**.
車子故障。

↦ The plan has **broken down**.
計劃失敗。

☐☐ **lay down** 放下；寫下

↦ She **lays** the child **down** gently.
她輕輕地將小孩放下。

↦ **Lay** it **down** on paper so everyone understands better.
用紙寫下來，讓每個人更容易明白。

英文第三對怨偶的背離：Up & Down介詞片語

☐☐ **up to** 從事；正在做

>→ What is he **up to**?

　　他在忙什麼？

>→ What are you **up to**?

　　你正在做什麼？

☐☐ **up to**＋人　由（～人）負責

>→ It's all **up to you**.

　　這全由你決定（負責）。

☐☐ **call up** 打電話給～

>→ Please, **call** me **up** tonight at my office.

　　今晚請打電話到辦公室給我。

>→ Did anyone **call** me **up**?

　　有沒有人打電話給我？

>→ I will **call** you **up** tomorrow.

　　明天我會打電話給你。

>→ **Call** me **up** at seven in the morning.

　　早上七點打電話給我。

☐☐ **fill up** 充滿；填滿

>→ Let me **fill up** your glass, Mr. Liu.

　　劉先生，讓我幫你杯子加滿水。

>→ I'm **filled up**. I can't drink any more.

　　我肚子填滿了，再也喝不下去了。

英文第三對怨偶的背離：Up & Down 介開片語

□□ fix up 安排；和解

→ Can you **fix** him **up** for the night？
你能給他安排晚上的住處嗎？

→ They **fixed up** a quarrel. 他們解決了爭端。

□□ hurry up 趕快

→ **Hurry up,** or we'll miss the train.
快點，要不然要趕不上火車了。

□□ wrap up 包裝

→ Do you want me to **wrap** it **up** as a gift？
你要我把它當做禮物包起來嗎？

→ Would you mind **wrapping** it **up** as a gift？
請把它像禮物一樣包起來，好嗎？

□□ upside down 倒置

→ He was reading a paper **upside down.**
他把新聞倒過來看。

□□ down and out 窮困潦倒；垮了

→ Once a very rich man, he is now **down and out.**
他曾是一個很有錢的人，現在垮了。

□□ down to the wire 時間快盡；幾乎用盡（破產）

→ Bob is **down to the wire** on his project.
鮑伯的計劃期限快到了。

→ We are really **down to the wire.**
我們真的快破產了。

英文第三對怨偶的背離: Up & Down 介詞片語

❖ 精通 up & down 的其他用法!

☐☐ **back up** 支持;撐腰

☐☐ **bring up** 養育成人

⇨ He was brought up to be a doctor.

他長大要當醫生。

☐☐ **build up** 建立;加強

⇨ He has built up an excellent business.

他建立了一個成就非凡的事業。

☐☐ **catch up with** 趕上

⇨ I will soon catch up with you. 我馬上就會趕上你。

☐☐ **clear up** 放晴;清理

⇨ The sky has cleared up. 天空放晴了。

⇨ Clear up your desk a bit. 請稍微整理一下你的書桌。

＊ clean up 清掃

☐☐ **cut up** 切碎;嚴酷批評 ＊ cut up into 衣服裁剪成～

☐☐ **dress up** 盛裝

☐☐ **follow up** 緊追不捨;乘機行動

☐☐ **grow up** 長大

⇨ I grew up in the country. 我在鄉下長大。

☐☐ **hold up** 舉起;停止

⇨ He held up his hands. 他舉起雙手。

⇨ He is holding up her work.

他停止她的工作。

英文第三對怨偶的背離：Up&Down介閞片語

☐☐ **live up to** 依～生活

⇨ He lives up to his income.

他依靠收入來生活。

☐☐ **lock up** 鎖牢

⇨ Lock up the door. 把門鎖好。

⇨ She was locked up in a room. 她被關在一個房間裏。

☐☐ **look＋up＋物** 查閱～

⇨ Look up this word in the dictionary.

從字典裏查一下這個單字。

☐☐ **look＋人＋up** 訪問

⇨ Look me up next time you are in Taipei.

下次上台北要來拜訪我。

☐☐ **look up to** 尊敬

⇨ We look up to him. 我們崇敬他。

⊠ look down upon 輕視

☐☐ **mix up** 相混

⇨ Mix them up. 把它們混合。

＊ mix up A with B　A中混合進B

＊ be mixed up with 和下流之事有關

・He is mixed up with something shabby. 他牽扯上了不名譽的事情。

☐☐ **pack up** （機器）壞掉；停止；死

☐☐ **sit up** 徹夜不眠；沒睡

⇨ I sat up all night. 我整晚沒睡。

⇨ sit up at work 徹夜工作

英文第三對怨偶的背離：Up & Down 介詞片語

☐☐ **pick up** 拾起；偶得；恢復；鼓起勇氣；搭載

　　⇨ I picked up a purse in the street.
　　　我在街上撿到一個皮包。

　　⇨ Can you pick it up?
　　　你能幫我撿起來嗎？

　　⇨ He is beginning to pick up his health again.
　　　他又開始恢復健康了。

　　⇨ We'll stop at the Hilton Hotel and pick up Mr. Patrick.
　　　我們將會在希爾頓飯店停車搭載派翠克先生。

☐☐ **roll up** 積累

　　⇨ His debts were rolling up. 他債台高築。

　　＊ pitched and rolled 左右搖晃
　　・ The ship pitched and rolled. 船身左右搖擺晃動。

☐☐ **set up** 設立；從事

　　⇨ He set up a business. 他從商。

　　⇨ Let's set up a sign here.
　　　讓我們在這裏設一個標示。

　　⇨ He set himself up in life. 他自我創業。

　　＊ set up as 做～行業起家；開業　set up for 裝出～樣子
　　・ He sets up for learning. 他裝出一副很有學問的樣子。

☐☐ **shut up** 關閉

　　⇨ shut up shop 關店

　　⇨ We will shut up our store on Saturday.
　　　我們的店將在星期六關門。

　　＊ shut out 阻止進入

英文第三對怨偶的背離：Up & Down 介開片語

☐☐ **turn up** 向上彎；轉亮（大聲）一點
⇨ Turn up more. 向上彎一點。
⇨ Turn the radio up a little. 收音機開大聲一點。
反 turn down 轉弱一點

☐☐ **warm up** 暖身運動
⇨ You start warming up now.
你現在開始暖身運動。

☐☐ **wipe up** 徹底消滅

☐☐ **work up** （憑努力）逐漸建立；煽動；精心製作
⇨ We must work up a reputation.
我們必須逐漸建立聲譽。

☐☐ **write up** 描寫；為文讚揚

☐☐ **burn down** 燒毀
⇨ His house was burnt down. 他的房子燒毀了。

☐☐ **cut down** 砍倒；縮減
⇨ Let's cut down our expenses.
讓我們縮減開支。

☐☐ **drink down** 喝下
⇨ Drink it down. 把它喝下。

☐☐ **look down upon** 輕視 反 look up to 尊重

☐☐ **mark down** 減價
⇨ They mark down goods at that shop. 那家商店貨品減價。
反 mark up 加價；漲價

英文第三對怨偶的背離：Up & Down 介詞片語

☐ **quiet down** 安靜下來

⇨ Quiet down, please. 請安靜。

☐ **run down** 疲倦；往下跑；撞倒；尋找

⇨ You look quite run down.

你看起來相當疲倦。

⇨ We ran down the hill. 我們跑下山丘。

☐ **set down** 放下；卸下

⇨ Set it down there. 把它放在那邊。

☐ **settle down** 定居；安頓下來

⇨ She's married and settled down now.

她結婚了，現在安頓下來。

☐ **shut down** 關閉；停止　＊ shut down on 抑止；阻止

☐ **sit down** 坐下

＊ sit down to 就位

・ She sat down to the piano. 她就鋼琴位置坐下

・ Shall we sit down to dinner？我們可以就位用晚餐了嗎？

☐ **wash down** 沖洗

☐ **write down** 寫下；以文字詆毀

⇨ Please write down your name and address.

請寫下姓名和地址。

☐ **down-to-earth** 實際的

⇨ I like him. He is a down-to-earth man.

我喜歡他，他是一個實際的人。

4.In & Out 介詞

英文第四對冤家的對立

從外到內的 in，由內而外的 out

有一個很有趣的英文猜謎遊戲,是這樣問的:*How many hairs are there in a cat's tail*?(貓的尾巴裏有幾根毛?)這是考別人對 in a cat's tail 中 in 的文字了解。按照字面解釋,in 是「裏面」的意思,所以,答案是:*None, they are all outside.*(一根也沒有,全在外面。)

In 是「在～之中」的意思,如果畫一個框,就是指在那個框框以內的空間、時間、狀態等等。

在前面提到 on 是指接觸表面,有①接近②方向③支撐④倚靠⑤對象⑥狀態的進行等意思。而 in 則有①場所②時間③條件的限定④狀態等含意,讀者可以對照比較之。如果能夠分別 in 是表示「在～之中」、on 是表示「與物相接的部分」、to 是「方向」以及表時間的 in 是「在～,在～完了時」、within 是「以內」、after 是「以後」,就很容易背好相關的介詞片語。

1. Please come *in*. 請進。

2. Western clothes are easier to work *in* than Chinese clothes.
   西方的服裝比中國式服裝**穿起來**更容易作活。

3. Are your parents *in* now? 你的父母現在**在**嗎?

　　另外，in 還有以下必須注意的用法。Write in pencil（用鉛筆寫），如果改用 with 時，必須加不定冠詞 a 在前面，如 with a pencil。

　　Out 和 in 相反，是由內往外的意思。電話中，對方要找的人不在時，可回答："He's out for the day."（他今天整天都在外面。）或 "He is out of town on business."（他出差出去了。）或者 "He's gone to Taichung on business."（他剛剛出差去台中了。）等諸如此類的談法。

　　和介系詞不同，副詞後不接受詞，而必須去修飾動詞（verbs）、副詞（adverbs）、形容詞（adjectives）。然而在此之前所敘述的介系詞和副詞，幾乎都是表示方向的字。

溫習一下 in 的用法！

1. 表示**位置、場所**，「**在～之中（內）**」

　　例：We stayed in the house.（我們留在屋子裏。）

2. 表示**一段時間、時期**

　　例：(1) I was born in May.（我在五月出生。）

　　　　(2) I'll be back in a moment.（我馬上回來。）

3. 表示「**在～狀態；以～方法**」

　　例：(1) They marched in high spirits.（他們精神昂揚向前邁進。）

　　　　(2) He insisted on doing it in this way.（他堅持以此方法來做。）

4. 表示（**服裝、衣著**）**之穿著**

　　例：Students are dressed in uniform.（學生穿著制服。）

5. 表示「**職業；活動**」

　　例：I majored in Economics.（我主修經濟。）

6. 表示「**性質、能力**」

　　例：He has nothing of the hero in him.（他沒有英雄氣概。）

7. 表示**表達的方法、媒介、工具、材料等**

例：They speak in English.（他們講英文。）

溫習一下 out 的用法！

1. 表示**位置、運動方向**，「**向外，在外面**」

例：We went out for a walk.（我們出外散步。）

2. 表示「**消失；完結**」

例：(1) I can't wash the stains out.（我無法把污跡洗掉。）

(2) The fire has burned out.（火已經燒完了。）

3. 表示「**出現；公開；暴露（秘密）；綻放**」

例：(1) The secret is out.（秘密洩露了。）

(2) A rock stuck out of the water.（一塊岩石突出水面。）

(3) The flowers are out.（花開了。）

4. 表示「**完全地；徹底地**」

例：I was tired out.（我精疲力盡了。）

5. **強調距離之遠**

例：My brother lives out in the country.

（我弟弟住在很遠的鄉下。）

6. 表示「**失業**」、「**失勢**」

例：(1) He was voted out at the election.（他落選了。）

(2) The Democrats are out.（民主黨下台了。）

7. 表示「**錯誤**」

例：Your guess is a long way out.（你的猜測差太遠了。）

　　以上是我們對 in 和 out 的基本介紹，相信您一定很快就能掌握住意思。

英文第四對冤家的對立：in介詞片語

◆ 給您最精彩的 in 看！

☐ **in a hurry** 匆忙的

  → Why are you **in** such **a hurry**？你為何如此地匆忙？

☐ **in advance** 事先的；預先的

  → Please make your reservations one week **in advance**.
    請在一週之前預定好。

  → All the seats are sold **in advance**.
    所有座位是預先訂購的。

☐ **in black and white** 見於書面文字

  → Here it is, all **in black and white**.
    這裏是全部的書面說明。

☐ **in case** 倘使；如果

  → **In case** of rain telephone me. 如果下雨,打電話給我。

☐ **in charge of** 負責管理

  → I am **in charge of** the third-year class.
    我負責管理三年級學生。

  → Who's **in charge of** this section？ 誰負責管理這個地區？

☐ **in fact** 事實上

  → He is a scholar by name, not **in fact**.
    名義上,他是一位學者,事實上不是。

☐ **in front of** 在～之前

  → I will wait for you **in front of** the school.
    我會在學校前面等你。

英文第四對冤家的對立：In 介詞片語

☐☐ **in hand** 在手中

⟶ I still have some money **in hand**.
我仍有一些錢在手中。

☐☐ **in no time** 立即；馬上

⟶ Let me know **in no time** when he comes.
當他來的時候馬上通知我。

☐☐ **in order to V** 為了～

⟶ I rose early **in order to** catch the first train.
我早起是為了搭第一班火車。

☐☐ **in the air** （謠言）流傳的

⟶ There are rumors **in the air**. 謠言滿天飛。

☐☐ **in the street** 在街上

⟶ I met him **in the street**.
我在街上碰到他。

☐☐ **in time for** 及時

⟶ I got up early to be **in time for** the train.
我早起是為了及時趕上火車。

☐☐ **drop in** 不預期的拜訪

⟶ Let's **drop in** on the Alans .
讓我們去拜訪艾倫一家人。

☐☐ **major in** 主修；專攻

⟶ What did you **major in** at college ?
你大學主修什麼？

英文第四對冤家的對立：In 介詞片語

❖ 按字母順序快速學習 in 的用法！

☐☐ **in a sense** 從某意上說　* in all senses 從各方面來看

☐☐ **in addition to** 除～之外

☐☐ **in advance** 預先　* pay in advance 預先支付

☐☐ **in any case** 無論如何；一定

☐☐ **in charge of** 負責管理

☐☐ **in fashion** 流行
　　⇨ A black coat is in fashion this winter.
　　　今年冬天流行黑色外套。

☐☐ **in general** 一般的　反 in particular 特定的

☐☐ **in itself** 本來；本質上　* by itself 獨自；單獨

☐☐ **in need** 窮困

☐☐ **in need of** 需要
　　⇨ She is in need of help. 她需要幫助。

☐☐ **in place of** 代替

☐☐ **in turn** 依順序　* by turns 輪流；on the turn 正在轉變

☐☐ **in search of** 搜尋

☐☐ **in spite of** 不顧；置之不理

☐☐ **in the long run** 結局

☐☐ **in the world** 世界上；到底；究竟

☐☐ **in vain** 白費心力；無效的
　　⇨ It was in vain that we protested. 我們的抗議是白費心力。

英文第四對冤家的對立：Out 介詞片語

◆ 看看 out 的流行用法！

☐☐ **out of date** 落伍

➡ This book is a little **out of date**.
　　這本書有些落伍了。

☐☐ **out of fashion** 不流行

➡ It's already **out of fashion**.
　　這已經不流行了。

☐☐ **out of order** 故障

➡ The telephone is **out of order**, Mr. Chen.
　　陳先生，電話故障了。

☐☐ **out of order** 雜亂；故障

➡ His room is always **out of order**.
　　他的房間總是亂七八糟。

➡ Our TV is **out of order**.
　　我們的電視故障了。

☐☐ **out of the question** 不可能的

➡ We can't go in this weather; it is **out of the question**.
　　無疑的，這種天氣是不可能出去的。

☐☐ **out of sight** 看不見；離開視線

➡ The steamer is now **out of sight**.
　　汽艇現在已看不到了。

➡ His car soon went **out of sight**.
　　他的車子馬上駛離我們的視線。

英文第四對冤家的對立：**Out 介詞片語**

❖ 按字母順序速瞄一下 out 的說法！

☐☐ **break out** 發生

⇨ AIDS has broken out. 愛滋病發生了。

☐☐ **call out** 叫出去

⇨ He called me out. 他把我叫出去。

☐☐ **carry out** 達成；實現

⇨ He carried out all his aims. 他達成了他所有的目標。

☐☐ **find out** 發現；猜到〔謎底等〕；了解；想出

☐☐ **hold out** 伸出；主張；不讓接近；忍受；不認輸

⇨ He held out his hand. 他伸出手。

☐☐ **look out** 注意；小心

⇨ Look out for the wild dog! 小心惡犬！

☐☐ **out of** 在～外面；從～當中；由於～；超出

☐☐ **out of doors** 戶外

☐☐ **out of place** 不適當　圜 in place 適當

☐☐ **out of sight** 看不見　圜 in sight 看見

☐☐ **pick out** 選拔

☐☐ **run out** 耗盡；用完

☐☐ **run out of** 耗盡

⇨ He ran out of breath. 他斷氣了。　＊ run out on＋人　背棄

☐☐ **set out** 出發；試圖；陳列

⇨ They set out for London. 他們向倫敦出發。

☐☐ **work out** 解決；努力獲致；計劃

● 英文片語正誤用法 ●

♤ **make faces**

別對我**扮鬼臉**。

→ Stop making the faces at me. 《誤》

→ Stop making faces at me. 《正》

♤ **take pains**

他的妻子**下了一番苦功**去準備宴會。

→ His wife took a great pain with the preparations
  for the party. 《誤》

→ His wife took great pains with the preparations
  for the party. 《正》

♤ **consist**

會議**由**三個人**組成**。

→ The committee was consisted of three members.《誤》

→ The committee consisted of three members. 《正》

♤ **perish**

所有軍隊都**死於**那場戰爭。

→ All of the troops were perished in that battle. 《誤》

→ All of the troops perished in that battle. 《正》

♤ **superior to**

陸先生的車子**優於**他兒子的車。

→ Mr. Lu's car is superior than his son's. 《誤》

→ Mr. Lu's car is superior to his son's. 《正》

PART 6

肢體聯想記憶法
從頭到腳都是有趣的語言訊息！

● **肢體聯想記憶法的內容** —— 配合趣味的插圖，涵括人
體各部位引伸而出的慣用
語及口語，易學好用，難
以忘懷。

特色 —— 由自己的肢體名稱，運用
到相關片語中，充分發揮
您的想像力。

目的 —— 沒有負擔，字典就在身上，
方便記憶，一推即懂。

要訣 —— 圖文並茂，想到就說，輕
鬆掌握各種動作的訊息。

1.肢體相關趣味片語

eyebrow （眉）

☐☐ **knit the eyebrows** 皺眉頭

cheek （頰）

☐☐ **give cheek** 說無恥話

mouth （口）

☐☐ **from hand to mouth**
　　度日艱難；僅足糊口

☐☐ **from mouth to mouth**
　　一個傳一個

♤ *He doesn't knit the eyebrows.*

finger （指）

☐☐ **work** *one's* **fingers to the**
　　bone 非常努力的工作

thumb （大姆指）

☐☐ **all thumbs**
　　笨手笨腳的

☐☐ **thumb of gold** 搖錢樹

♤ *He is all thumbs.*

head （頭）

☐☐ **head up** 領頭；加頂

☐☐ **head back** 返回

☐☐ **head first** 頭在前；匆忙的

☐☐ **from head to foot** 從頭到腳

☐☐ **head on** 正面衝突

☐☐ **have a good head for business**
有商業頭腦

face （臉）

☐☐ **face to face** 面對面；面臨

☐☐ **face the face** 進入社會

☐☐ **face the music** 勇於面對艱苦；
接受處罰

☐☐ **face out** 以厚顏取勝；堅持到底

☐☐ **pull a face at** 給～壞臉色看；
拉長臉

☐☐ **on the face of it** 就表面看

eye （眼）

☐☐ **have an eye for** 對～有鑑賞力

☐☐ **have an eye on** 盯著～看

teeth （牙）

☐☐ **set teeth** 咬緊牙關；立下決心

neck （頸）

☐☐ **neck and neck**
（賽跑時）並肩齊驅

arm（手臂）

☐☐ **arm in arm** 手牽手

hand （手）

☐☐ **hand down** 遺留；傳下

☐☐ **on the other hand** 另一方面

☐☐ **have a good hand for** 擅長～

☐☐ **old hand at**（be an）
在～是老手

☐☐ **hand out** 交給

☐☐ **hand over** 轉讓

☐☐ **change hands** 更換人手

body（身軀）

☐☐ **body and soul** 專心一意

heart（心）

☐☐ **have a heart** 憐憫

back（背）

☐☐ **back and forth** 前後來回

☐☐ **back out of** 食言；因難而退

☐☐ **back up** 支持；使倒退

☐☐ **go back on** 背叛

☐☐ **back out** （車子）倒退

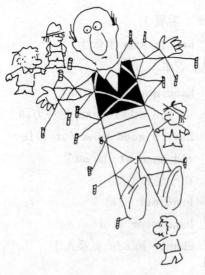

hip（臀）；**thigh**（股）

☐☐ **smite hip and thigh** 不留情地
攻擊；打屁股

leg（腿）

☐☐ **take to** *one's* **legs** 逃走

☐☐ **be all legs** （人）長得過高而細瘦

foot（足）

☐☐ **set out on foot** 開始；着手

☐☐ **at** *a person's* **feet** 服從～人

toe（脚趾）

☐☐ **from top to toe** 徹頭徹尾

2. 肢體動作實用片語

① **look** （看）

- ☐☐ **look after** 看顧；照料
- ☐☐ **look ahead** 預測；未雨綢繆
- ☐☐ **look around** 四處張望
- ☐☐ **look at** 注視；盯
- ☐☐ **look away** 轉目他視
- ☐☐ **look back on** 回顧
- ☐☐ **look down on**
- ☐☐ **look down upon**　　輕視
- ☐☐ **look for** 尋找
- ☐☐ **look forward to** 期望；期待
- ☐☐ **look in**（on）順道訪問
- ☐☐ **look into** 調查
- ☐☐ **look like A** 看起來像A（君）
- ☐☐ **look on** 旁觀
- ☐☐ **look on A as B**
- ☐☐ **look upon A as B**　　視A為B
- ☐☐ **look out**（for）注意查看
- ☐☐ **look over** 校閱；看過一遍
- ☐☐ **look through** 透過～看；看穿
- ☐☐ **look to A for B** 依賴A為了B
- ☐☐ **look up** 查閱；尋找；改進；探訪
- ☐☐ **look up to** 尊敬；崇敬

② **hold** （握）

☐☐ **hold good** 有效

⇨ The ticket holds good for 2 days.
這張票有效期是兩天。

☐☐ **hold true** 適用

☐☐ **hold still** 靜止不動

☐☐ **hold back** 克制

☐☐ **hold** *one's* **breath** 屏息

⇨ He watched the match holding his breath.
他屏息地看著火柴。

☐☐ **hold** *one's* **own** 堅持立場

⇨ The patient is holding his own. 病人堅持自己立場。

☐☐ **hold** *one's* **tongue** 閉嘴；不要說話

③ **catch** （抓）

☐☐ **catch cold** 感冒 同 have a cold

☐☐ **catch sight of** 看見 反 lose sight of

☐☐ **catch fire** 著火

☐☐ **catch a glimpse of** 一瞥

⇨ I caught a glimpse of her face. 我匆匆一瞥她的臉。

☐☐ **catch on** 理解；流行

⇨ I hope it catches on. 我希望它流行。

④ **answer** （回答）

☐☐ **answer for** 對～有責任

 ⇨ You have to answer for what you said.
  你必須對你所說的負責。

☐☐ **answer the purpose** 適合；可用作～

⑤ **ask** （問）

☐☐ **ask after** 問候；問安

 ⇨ Don't forget to ask after your uncle.
  別忘了向你叔叔問安。

☐☐ **ask a person in** 叫某人進來

 ⇨ Don't leave him standing on the doorstep, ask him in!
  別讓他站在門口的階梯，叫他進來！

⑥ **beat** （打）

☐☐ **beat back** 擊退

 ⇨ We attacked the enemy but were beaten back.
  我們攻擊敵人但被擊退了。

☐☐ **beat it** 滾開

 ⇨ The policeman told the boys to beat it.
  這警察叫這些小孩滾開。

⑦ **break** （折斷）

☐ **break away**（**from**）拆毀；突然離開

⇨ They broke away from the party to form their own.

他們脫離黨自組黨團。

☐ **break down** 破壞；壞掉；失敗

⇨ The peace negotiations have broken down.

和平談判失敗。

☐ **break in** 闖入；插嘴

⇨ He broke in while we were talking.

正當我們談話時他插嘴進來。

☐ **break into** 闖入

⇨ The thief broke into the office during the night.

小偷在夜裏闖入辦公室。

☐ **break off** 突然停止

☐ **break out** 發生；逃走

⇨ Two prisoners have broken out.

兩個囚犯逃走了。

☐ **break through** 突破

☐ **break up** 停止；散開；弄碎

☐ **break with** 與～絕交

⑧ **bring** （攜帶）

☐☐ **bring about** 使發生；致使

⇒ Gambling has brought about his ruin.

賭博使他傾家蕩產。

☐☐ **bring forward** 提出

⇒ Will you bring forward this matter at the next meeting?

請在下次會議提出這問題好嗎？

☐☐ **bring home to** 使明瞭

⇒ The policeman's words brought the seriousness of the affair home to me.

警察的話使我明瞭事情的嚴重性。

☐☐ **bring in** 使賺到；介紹

⇒ His writing only brings in a small income.

寫作只使他賺到一小筆錢。

☐☐ **bring through** 拯救

⇒ His illness was serious but the doctors managed to bring him through.

他病得很重，但醫生打算救他。

☐☐ **bring under** 降服；制服

⇒ The rebellion was soon brought under.

叛亂很快被制服。

⑨ **call** （喊叫）

☐☐ **call down** 斥責

⇨ Don't call her down for that mistake.
不要爲那錯誤斥責她。

☐☐ **call for** 迎；接

⇨ We'll call for you on our way to the concert.
在往音樂會的途中，我們會去接你。

☐☐ **call someone names** 侮辱；辱罵～人

⇨ He lost his temper and began calling me names.
他發脾氣開始辱罵我。

⑩ **carry** （提；搬）

☐☐ **carry away** 感動；使入迷

⇨ She was carried away by his enthusiasm.
她被他的熱忱所感動。

☐☐ **carry off** 誘拐；得〔獎〕

⇨ The kidnappers carried off the child.
綁匪將小孩拐走。

☐☐ **carry on** 繼續；行爲

⇨ He carried on his painting for many years.
他繼續作畫多年。

⇨ I don't like the way she carries on.
我不喜歡她做事的方式。

⑪ **cast** （ 投 ；扔 ；擲 ）

☐ **cast aside** 拋棄 ；排除
⇨ John cast aside his books and turned on the TV.
約翰丟下書本打開電視 。

☐ **cast beyond the moon** 任意推測

☐ **cast out** 擲下 ；丟棄
⇨ We cannot cast out so much money for a risky invest-
ment. 我們不能擲下這麼多錢在多風險的投資上 。

☐ **cast a vote** 投票表決

⑫ **close** （ 關 ；近 ）

☐ **close at hand** 在附近

☐ **close by** 很近

☐ **close call** 千鈞一髮

☐ **close down** 關門

☐ **close in on** 圍住 ；迫近
⇨ The enemy troops closed in on the city.
敵軍包圍了那城市 。

☐ **close out** 減價脫售

☐ **close up** 密集在一起 ；停業
⇨ The line of policemen closed up to prevent anyone
getting through. 警察聚集成一列防止任何人穿過 。

⑬ **draw** （拉；牽）

☐☐ **draw back** 退回

☐☐ **draw in** 〔日〕縮短
　　⇨ After September the days seem to draw in very quickly. 九月後白天似乎黑得特別快。

☐☐ **draw interest** 獲利

☐☐ **draw** *one's* **last breath** 去世
　　⇨ The dying man's eyes closed; he had drawn his last breath. 瀕死的人閉上了眼睛，嚥下最後的一口氣。

☐☐ **draw the sword** 宣戰；開戰
　　⇨ The king declared that he would never be the first to draw the sword.
　　這國王聲稱他決不作第一個宣戰的人。

⑭ **drop** （掉落）

☐☐ **drop in** 順便造訪
　　⇨ If you are free, won't you drop in and have a cup of coffee ? 你如果有空，何不過來喝杯咖啡呢？

☐☐ **drop off** 漸漸減少；不知不覺睡著
　　⇨ He was so tired he dropped off in front of the television. 他太累了，不知不覺在電視機前睡著了。

☐☐ **drop out of** 退出；離去
　　⇨ He dropped out of this tough world.
　　他退出這個無情的世界。

⑮ **eat** （吃）

☐☐ **eat away** 侵蝕

　　⇨ The rust ate away the metal.
　　　　金屬生銹了。

☐☐ **eat in** 在家裏吃　囮 **eat out**

☐☐ **eat into** 侵蝕

　　⇨ These travels are eating into my pocket.
　　　　這些旅行蝕了我的老本。

☐☐ **eat** *one's* **heart out** 使人極度悲痛

☐☐ **eat** *one's* **word** 食言

☐☐ **eat** *one's* **head off** 吃太多

☐☐ **eat up** 吃光；使著迷

　　⇨ He was eaten up with pride.
　　　　他被驕傲沖昏了頭。

⑯ **fall** （跌倒）

☐☐ **fall among** 遇到

　　⇨ The traveller fell among thieves.
　　　　這旅行者遇到盜賊。

☐☐ **fall asleep** 睡著

☐☐ **fall away** 消退

　　⇨ My strength began to fall away.
　　　　我的力量開始消退。

☐☐ **fall back** 後退

> ⇨ As our army advanced, the enemy fell back.
> 當我們部隊前進，敵軍後退了。

☐☐ **fall back on** 依靠

> ⇨ If meat gets too expensive, we can fall back on fish.
> 如果肉太貴，我們可以靠吃魚。

☐☐ **fall behind** 落後；逾期

☐☐ **fall for** 戀慕

> ⇨ He always falls for a pretty face.
> 他經常戀慕漂亮臉蛋的人。

☐☐ **fall ill** 生病

☐☐ **fall into line** 排隊

☐☐ **fall off** 減少

> ⇨ Radio audiences have fallen off. 收音機的聽衆已減少。

☐☐ **fall out** 紛爭；發生；〔軍〕離隊

☐☐ **fall short of** 缺乏；未達到

☐☐ **fall through** 落空

> ⇨ Our plans for a picnic fell through.
> 我們野餐的計劃落空。

☐☐ **fall upon** 攻擊

> ⇨ We fell upon the enemy troops while they were sleeping. 我們趁敵軍睡覺時攻擊。

⑰ **feel** （摸）

☐☐ **feel after** 摸索而找

⇨ What are you feeling after? 你在找什麼？

☐☐ **feel for** 同情；體諒

⇨ We all feel for you in this crisis.

在這次危機中，我們都很同情你。

☐☐ **feel in** *one's* **bones** 直覺

⇨ I felt it in my bones that she would not survive.

我直覺到她不能倖免於難。

☐☐ **feel like** 想要

☐☐ **feel** *one's* *pulse* 量脈搏

☐☐ **feel** *one's* **way** 小心謹慎行動

⇨ The soldiers felt their way through the fields.

士兵們小心謹慎地穿過田地。

☐☐ **feel up to** *one's* **work** 感覺承當得了工作。

⇨ I'm much better today; I even feel up to going to
work. 今天我感到好多了，甚至覺得自己可以去工作了。

⑱ **hear** （聽）

☐☐ **hear from** 收到信

☐☐ **hear out** 聽完

⇨ She didn't even hear me out before she said no.

還沒聽我說完，她就一口拒絕了。

⑲ **hit** （打）

☐☐ **hit below the belt** 卑鄙行為

☐☐ **hit it off with** 志趣相投

⇨ I hit it off well with Joe.
我和喬志趣相投 。

☐☐ **hit the bottom** 用完

☐☐ **hit the ceiling** 暴跳如雷

⇨ When the manager found the error, he hit the ceiling.
當這經理發現這錯誤時，他暴跳如雷 。

☐☐ **hit the mark** 成功

⇨ Fellows, it looks as if we are going to hit the mark.
伙伴們，看來我們似乎快成功了 。

☐☐ **hit or miss** 不管成敗

☐☐ **hit the nail on the head** 說中 ; 做對事情

⇨ You called him a miser and hit the nail on the head.
你叫他吝嗇鬼眞是一語命中 。

⑳ **laugh** （笑）

☐☐ **laugh at** 〔聽見〕而笑 ; 嘲笑

☐☐ **laugh away** 付之一笑

☐☐ **laugh in** *one's* **sleeve** 竊笑

⇨ We laughed in our sleeves when she began to sing.
當她開始唱歌時 ，我們偷偷竊笑 。

㉑ **lay** （置放）

☐☐ **lay a finger on** 正確指出
⇒ I dare not lay a finger on his mistake.
我不敢指出他的錯誤。

☐☐ **lay aside** 停止；放棄；貯藏
⇒ She laid aside her work to answer the telephone.
她放下工作去接電話。
⇒ He laid aside a large amount of money for his son's education.
他儲蓄了一大筆錢給兒子當教育費。

☐☐ **lay down** 使躺下；貯藏；捐軀；規定
⇒ Lay down the baby.
把小孩放下來躺著。
⇒ Many patriots laid down their lives for their country.
許多愛國者爲國捐軀。

☐☐ **lay eyes on** 看見

☐☐ **lay in** 貯藏　同 lay up

☐☐ **lay off** 解雇
⇒ The factory laid off several workers recently.
這家工廠最近解雇了幾名員工。

☐☐ **lay out** 花費；設計
⇒ He laid out a large amount of money for the car.
他花了一大筆錢買了那輛車。

㉒ **move** （移；搬運）

☐☐ **move heaven and earth** 盡最大努力

☐☐ **move in on** 向～進攻

⇨ The soldiers moved in on that castle.
士兵們向城堡進攻。

☐☐ **move up** 晉升

⇨ Dr. Lee was moved up from an associate to a full
professor. 李博士由副教授晉升教授。

☐☐ **move in** 遷入　囻 **move out**

⇨ The new tenants will move in tomorrow.
新房客明天將會搬進來。

㉓ **pick** （挑；探）

☐☐ **pick at** 以指彈；慢慢吃

☐☐ **pick off** 一個一個地射

⇨ The hunter picked off the birds as they flew by.
當鳥飛過時獵人一隻一隻地射。

☐☐ **pick on** 挑選；揶揄

⇨ We picked on Mr. Lee to be our speaker.
我們選李先生爲我們的發言人。

☐☐ **pick up** 搭載；加速

⇨ The train picked up speed.
火車加速。

㉔ **play** （玩）

☐☐ **play along with** 與～合作
　　⇨ The best way to attain our goal is to play along with them.
　　　達成我們目標的最好方法就是與他們合作。

☐☐ **play at** 假裝；做事不認真

☐☐ **play ball with** 與～合作

☐☐ **play into the hands of** 中計；上當
　　⇨ By being careless, he played into the hands of his opponent. 由於不小心，他中了對手的計。

☐☐ **play** *one's* **cards right** 策略運用得當
　　⇨ The competition is strong, but if we play our cards right, we may yet win that contract.
　　　競爭非常激烈，但如果我們策略運用得當，或許還能贏得合同。

☐☐ **play safe** 小心；謹慎

☐☐ **play the fool** 行動愚蠢
　　⇨ It is about time he stopped playing the fool and began to settle down.
　　　這該是他結束愚蠢行動的時候，開始安定下來。

☐☐ **play the market** 玩股票

☐☐ **play up to** 〔俗〕諂媚；求寵
　　⇨ Mary is playing up to her employer.
　　　瑪麗向她的老闆求寵。

㉕ **pull** （拉；扯）

☐☐ **pull a boner** 犯下愚蠢的錯誤

⇨ You pulled a boner when you refused her invitation.
    你拒絕她的邀請就是犯了個愚蠢的錯誤。

☐☐ **pull a fast one** 搶先以做利己的事

☐☐ **pull down** 拆除；使降低

☐☐ **pull in** 勒緊；逮捕；抵達

⇨ The hungry man pulled in his belt.
    這飢餓的人勒緊他的褲帶。

⇨ The police pulled in four men who were gambling.
    警方逮捕了四名賭博的男子。

☐☐ **pull off** 脫掉；成功地達成

⇨ I never thought you'd pull the competition off.
    我從未想過你會成功地贏得這場比賽。

☐☐ **pull** *oneself* **together** 恢復正常能力

⇨ Don't be hysterical; pull yourself together.
    別再歇斯底里了，恢復正常吧！

☐☐ **pull over** 路邊停車

⇨ The policeman shouted, "Pull the car over to the
    curb." 那警察叫道：「把車停到路邊。」

☐☐ **pull strings** 運用私人影響力

☐☐ **pull up** 阻止；停止

㉖ **read** （讀）

☐☐ **read between the lines** 了解弦外之音

☐☐ **read out of** 自～逐出
　　⇨ Tim was read out of the party for violating its rules.
　　　提姆因違反黨規而被逐出政黨。

☐☐ **read through** 從頭到尾唸完

㉗ **run** （跑）

☐☐ **run around** 有外遇

☐☐ **run away with** 同～私奔

☐☐ **run down** 停止；疲勞
　　⇨ The watch has run down.
　　　手錶停了。
　　⇨ He is run down from overwork.
　　　他工作過度而累壞了。

☐☐ **run off** 印出
　　⇨ This machine will run off eighty copies per minute.
　　　這部機器每分鐘可印八十份。

☐☐ **run on** 繼續不停的討論

☐☐ **run through** 複習；花錢很快
　　⇨ He won much money at the races and ran through it
　　　in a week.
　　　他在賭馬時贏了許多錢，但在一個禮拜內便花光了。

㉘ **see** （看）

☐☐ **see about** 注意

⇨ I'll see about it. 我會注意它。

☐☐ **see eye to eye** 同意

☐☐ **see much of** 常碰面

⇨ I don't see much of you these days.

最近我很少看到你。

☐☐ **see** *someone* **off** 送行

⇨ We saw her off at the airport yesterday.

昨天我們到機場為她送行。

☐☐ **see red** 生氣；發怒

☐☐ **see stars** 眼冒金星

⇨ I saw stars when I hit my head against the door.

當我的頭撞到門時，眼睛直冒金星。

☐☐ **see through** 看透；看穿

⇨ I saw through the lawyer's trick and did not answer

him. 我看穿那律師的把戲，沒有回答他。

㉙ **sit** （坐）

☐☐ **sit in on** 參加

⇨ He sat in on the conference all morning.

他整個早上都在參加這會議。

☐☐ **sit on the fence** 騎牆，保持觀望。

㉚　**speak** （說）

☐☐　**speak for** 為～說情（講好話）

　⇨ He said that he was not speaking for himself but for the group which he represented.

　　他說他不是在為個人說好話，而是代表他的團體說話。

☐☐　**speak of** 值得一提

　⇨ I didn't think his performance was anything to speak of. 我不認為他的表演有什麼值得一提的地方。

☐☐　**speak out** 老實說出來

　⇨ Speak out. I want to hear exactly what you think.

　　老實說出來吧！我想聽聽你真正的想法。

☐☐　**speak up** 大聲說

㉛　**stand** （站立）

☐☐　**stand aside** 靠邊站

☐☐　**stand by** 旁觀；援助

　⇨ He always stood by his friends in difficult times.

　　當他的朋友有困難時，他總是伸出援手。

☐☐　**stand on** *one's* **own feet** 自立

☐☐　**stand up for** 抵抗；對抗

　⇨ The lawyer stood up for his clients.

　　律師為他的訴訟委託人辯護。

㉜ **talk** （說話）

☐☐ **talk big** 說大話

⇨ He likes to talk big as though he were a very important person.

他好說大話，儼然像是一位大人物。

☐☐ **talk into** 勸說

⇨ We finally talked father into buying a new car.

我們終於勸說老爸買輛新車。

☐☐ **talk** *one's* **head off** 向人喋喋不休

☐☐ **talk over** 討論

☐☐ **talk shop** 討論商務（生意）

☐☐ **talk to death** 以長篇演說扼殺（議案）

㉝ **think** （想）

☐☐ **think a lot of** 喜歡；尊敬

⇨ His friends think a lot of John.

他的朋友們很喜歡約翰。

☐☐ **think better of it** 再考慮一下

☐☐ **think it fit** 認為～適當

⇨ Apparently he thought it fit not to follow our advice in the matter. 顯然地，他認為此事不聽我們的勸告是對的。

☐☐ **think out** 想出

☐☐ **think up** 想起

㉞　**throw** （丟）

□□ **throw away** 丟棄

⇨ He threw those old magazines away.

他把這些舊雜誌丟掉。

□□ **throw cold water on** 潑冷水；使氣餒

⇨ We wanted an elaborate wedding, but father threw cold water on the idea.

我們想舉行一場精心設計的婚禮，可是老爸對這主意潑冷水。

□□ **throw in the sponge** 認輸　同 throw in the towel

⇨ Don't throw in the sponge. You may still win.

不要認輸，你仍可以贏的。

□□ **throw on** 匆匆穿上　反 throw off

⇨ He threw on his jacket and left the house.

他匆匆穿上夾克，離開屋子。

□□ **throw** *one's* **weight around** 專權；弄權

⇨ We don't like the way he throws his weight around.

我們都不喜歡他的弄權。

□□ **throw out** 被迫離去；否決（議案）

⇨ The noisy boys were thrown out of the theater.

吵鬧的小孩被逐出劇院。

□□ **throw up** 嘔吐

⇨ He threw up his breakfast.

他把吃的早餐吐出來了。

㉟ **walk** （走）

☐☐ **walk all over** 使喚

⇨ I have little respect for any man who lets his wife walk all over him.

我看不起一些被太太使喚的男人。

☐☐ **walk of life** 社會地位

⇨ He has come in contact with people from all walks of life.

他和來自社會各階層的人接觸。

☐☐ **walk off with** 偷走

⇨ Someone has walked off with my purse.

有人偷走我的皮包。

☐☐ **walk on air** 興奮

☐☐ **walk out on** 遺棄

⇨ Her husband walked out on her.

她的先生遺棄她。

㊱ **wear** （穿）

☐☐ **wear away** 磨損

☐☐ **wear off** 消滅

⇨ The effect of the drug wore off quickly.

藥效很快消失。

☐☐ **wear out** 筋疲力竭

3.其他生活慣用語

☐ **after all** 最後；畢竟
☐ **all over** 到處
☐ **as a rule** 通常
☐ **at sight** 看見
☐ **but for** ～ 如非～；若不是～
☐ **by luck** 靠運氣
☐ **care to** ～ 喜歡
☐ **close by** ～ 在～附近

☐ **for certain** 確定；證實
☐ **in turn** 依順序；必然也～
☐ **look to** ～ 照顧；注意；仰賴～
☐ **much less** 更談不上；甭提
☐ **may well** ～ 儘可～
☐ **occur to** ～ 使想到～
☐ **owe … to** ～ 負有～義務
☐ **sooner or later** 遲早

- □□ **submit to**～ 服從～
- □□ **at most** 最多～
- □□ **be born to**～ 天生註定～
- □□ **break out** 發生
- □□ **carry out** 實行；完成
- □□ **count on** 依賴；信賴
- □□ **fit for** 合適的
- □□ **on earth** 究竟

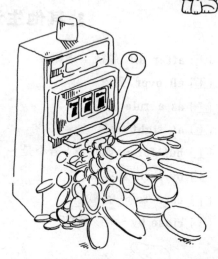

□□ **be good at** 精通～

He is good at figures. 他精於算術。

～ at tennis. 他精於打網球。

～ at golf. 他精於打高爾夫球。

～ at cooking. 他精於烹飪。

□□ **be good for** 對～有用處

He is good for nothing. 他一無用處。

He is good for something. 他有些用處。

☐☐ **call on** 請求；訪問

☐☐ **come back** 回來

☐☐ **come over** 訪問

☐☐ **get up** 起床

☐☐ **get along** 進展；前進

☐☐ **get along with** 與人相處

☐☐ **get out of** 逃出

☐☐ **get through** 完成

☐☐ **get by** 勉強及格；通過

☐☐ **get over** 痊癒

☐☐ **go on** 發生

☐☐ **go over** 複習

☐☐ **keep on** 繼續

☐☐ **look into** 調查

☐☐ **look for** 尋找

☐☐ **look out** 小心

☐☐ **look like** 肖似

☐☐ **make out** 成功

☐☐ **make sure of** 確定

☐☐ **run over** 輾過

☐☐ **run across** 偶然遇見

☐☐ **run into** 偶遇

☐☐ **show off** 炫耀

☐☐ **show up** 出現

♤ *Look out* !

- [ ] **look up** 查明
- [ ] **look over** 檢查
- [ ] **make up** 彌補
- [ ] **pick out** 選出
- [ ] **put off** 延期
- [ ] **put on** 穿上
- [ ] **put out** 熄滅
- [ ] **take off** 脫下

- [ ] **call up** 打電話
- [ ] **do over** 重覆做
- [ ] **fill out** 填滿
- [ ] **give back** 返回
- [ ] **give up** 投降；放棄
- [ ] **hand in** 交出
- [ ] **keep up** 維持
- [ ] **leave out** 省略

- [ ] **take up** 著手
- [ ] **take down** 記錄下來
- [ ] **talk over** 討論
- [ ] **try out** 精煉
- [ ] **turn in** 交給
- [ ] **turn off** 關掉
- [ ] **turn on** 打開
- [ ] **use up** 用盡

☐☐ **as a matter of fact** 事實上
　　同 in fact

☐☐ **as a result** 結果

☐☐ **as a whole** 全盤而論

☐☐ **as far as** 盡…所～

☐☐ **as follows** 如下所述

☐☐ **as it were** 換言之
　　同 so to speak ; in other
　　words

☐☐ **as long as** 只要
　　同 so long as ; if only

☐☐ **as of** 照情形看
　　⇨ As of now, there is no sign of improvement.
　　照目前情形看,沒有改善的跡象。

☐☐ **as such** 如此
　　⇨ I'm not a fool and I don't want to be treated as
　　such. 我不是笨蛋,我不想被如此對待。

☐☐ **as to** 至於
　　⇨ I have heard nothing more as to that matter.
　　至於那件事情我沒多聽到些什麼。

☐☐ **at a loss** 迷惘

☐☐ **at all times** 經常

☐☐ **at any cost** 不論任何代價
　　回 by all means

☐☐ **at any risk** 不管多危險

☐☐ **at fault** 做錯

☐☐ **at hand** 接近；在即
　　⇨ The examination is
　　　 close at hand.
　　　 考試在即。

☐☐ **at home in** 熟悉
　　⇨ He is at home in law.
　　　 他熟悉法律。

☐☐ **at issue** 爭論中
　　⇨ The question is at issue.
　　　 問題在爭論中。

☐☐ **at large** 逍遙法外
　　⇨ The escaped prisoner is still at large.
　　　 逃走的犯人仍逍遙法外。

☐☐ **by all means** 必定

⇨ By all means, come with us to dinner tonight.

今晚一定要來和我們吃晚飯。

☐☐ **by and by** 不久

⇨ It will rain by and by.

天不久就會下雨。

☐☐ **by and large** 一般而言

⇨ By and large, they did well in the performance.

一般而言他們表演得還不錯。

☐☐ **by chance** 偶然地;意外地

圓 by accident

☐☐ **by heart** 背誦;靠記憶

☐☐ **by means of** 藉～

☐☐ **by the way** 順便提及

⇨ By the way, Henry, did you have any lunch?

亨利,順便一提,你吃過午餐了嗎?

☐☐ **by way of** 經由

⇨ We will travel to Los Angeles by way of Tokyo.

我們經由東京到洛杉磯。

□□ **for all** 儘管　回 in spite of
⇨ For all his wealth, he is still unhappy.
儘管他有錢，他仍不快樂。

□□ **for ever and ever** 永遠
⇨ He said he will love her for ever and ever.
他說他將永遠愛著她。

□□ **for good** 永久

□□ **for all that** 儘管如此

□□ **for all the world** 的確

□□ **for life** 終生

□□ **for the present** 暫時地

□□ **for nothing** 免費的

□□ **for short** 簡稱

□□ **for the sake of** 為了～緣故

□□ **for the moment** 目前

□□ **for the purpose of** 為了～目的

□□ **for the time being** 暫時地
⇨ He lives with us for the time being.
他暫時和我們住在一起。

特輯（口俚語的妙用）
USEFUL MINI-PHRASES

big hand
鼓掌

⇨ "Here he is, Mr. George Michael. Let's give him a big hand."
「喬治・邁可先生，讓我們為他鼓掌。」

big mouth
長舌的人，大嘴巴

⇨ You are a big mouth! 你真是個大嘴巴！
⇨ If you open your big mouth, I'll beat you up. 你如果開口講話，我就揍你。

all thumbs
笨手笨腳

⇨ I'm all thumbs. Could you help me tie this knot?
我真是笨手笨腳的。你能幫我打這個結嗎？

bawl (one's) head off
哭得很大聲

⇨ The child bawled his head off when his mother hit him.
當他的母親揍他的時候，他哭得驚天動地。

blabber mouth
多嘴婆

⇨ Here comes the blabber mouth.
多嘴婆來了。

blood in one's eyes
生氣

⇨ "Who said I was angry?"
"Well, everybody said they could see blood in your eyes."
「誰說我生氣了?」
「每一個人都這麼說,他們可以看到你眼中的血絲。」

blood sucker(＝*leech*)
吸血鬼(指放高利貸的人)

⇨ You blood sucker, leave my father alone. 你這吸血鬼,別煩我爸爸。

blow your head off
打爛你的頭(用槍射)

⇨ If you say one more word, I'll blow your head off.
你再說一句,我就打爛你的頭。

bull's eye(＝*hit the bull's eye*)
對了;完全正確

⇨ "What's the capital of Italy?"
"Rome?"
"Bull's eye!"
「義大利的首都在哪裏?」
「羅馬?」
「完全正確!」

burn one's ears
叱責;責罵

⇨ If he really did it, I'm going to burn his ears.
如果他眞的幹了這事,我會罵他一頓。

by a hair(＝*just squeak by*)些微之差

⇨ We won the game by a hair.
我們險勝了對方。

cross (*one's*) **heart** (*and hope to die*) 發誓

⇨ I didn't tell your mother, cross my heart. 我沒有告訴你媽媽，我發誓。

＊有的人還一邊講一邊在心口畫個十字。

cry one's eyes out 哭腫了眼

⇨ After hearing the bad news, she cried her eyes out.
當她聽到那個壞消息之後，她哭腫了眼。

button one's lip 不開口；拒絕洩密

⇨ She buttons her lip.
她守口如瓶。

dry as a bone 形容東西很乾，沒有一點水份

⇨ It was raining outside my house but three blocks away the street was dry as a bone. 我家這兒在下雨，但三條街外却是乾乾的一滴雨也沒有。

eat (*one's*) **heart out** 羨慕死

⇨ If you meet Lisa's boyfriend, you will eat your heart out.
假如妳看到 Lisa 的男朋友，妳會羨慕死。

face the music 去面對不愉快的（責罰、挨罵）

⇨ If we are going to be punished, I don't want to face the music alone.
假如我們要受罰，我可不願一個人去承擔。

get (＝*have*) **cold feet** 害怕（腿軟）

⇨ When I have to see a doctor, I get cold feet.
每當我必須要去看醫生時，我總是很害怕。

⇨ He got cold feet right before his wedding day.
就在結婚的前一天，他感到非常害怕。

get (*one's*) **foot in the door** 邁入第一步

⇨ His new job at the company isn't high paying, but at least he got his foot in the door. 他在那家公司的新工作待遇不高，但至少進去了。

get off my back 少惹我

⇨ I'm not in a good mood, so get off my back. 我心情不好，少惹我。

get on (*one's*) **back** 找麻煩；催某人做事

⇨ I don't know why Mr. White always gets on my back.

不知爲什麼白先生老是找我的麻煩。

⇨ John always gets on his brother's back. 約翰老是催他弟弟做事。

give a hand 幫忙（指體力上的）

⇨ " Judy, give me a hand, will you ? Pass me that hammer."

「茱蒂，幫個忙好嗎?把那個鎚子遞給我。」

give (*someone*) **the finger** 伸出中指表示侮辱

⇨ That creep used to hang around my sister, but she gave him the finger, and told him to get lost.

那混蛋常常騷擾我妹妹，她伸出她的中指給他看，並叫他滾遠點。

* the finger 是指中指，在美國，伸出一隻中指指著人，表示 fuck 的意思。這是一個極爲粗野的動作，所以可別亂伸手指，小心挨揍！

(*have*) **got an eye** 打算要做；留意；有鑑賞力

⇨ He's got an eye to marry Helen. 他打算要娶海倫。

⇨ She hasn't got an eye to marry.
她還沒打算要結婚。

⇨ I've got an eye out for that book.
If I find it, I'll tell you. 我已經留
意那本書了。如果我發現,我會告訴你。

⇨ He has an eye for art.
他對藝術很有眼光。

greeted with open
arms 受到熱烈歡迎

⇨ When he went back to the school, he
was greeted with open arms.
他返回學校時,受到了熱烈的歡迎。

hands up 舉起手來
(搶刼時常用)

⇨ Hands up and don't move!
手舉起來,別動!

have a chip on (*one's*)
shoulder 憤世嫉俗;易動怒

⇨ He has a chip on his shoulder.
他很憤世嫉俗。

have a heart of gold
心地善良

⇨ I like Sandy, she has a heart of gold.
我喜歡珊蒂,她心地善良。

have diarrhea of the
mouth 話太多;太囉嗦

⇨ "Would you shut up? You've got
diarrhea of the mouth."
「你閉嘴好不好?你的話太多了。」
* diarrhea〔͵daɪə'riə〕*n.* 腹瀉

hit the nail on the
head
答對了;計劃很好

⇨ "I think the real reason he won't
change jobs is that he's afraid to
try something new."
"You hit the nail right on the head."

「我想他不肯換工作的眞正原因是因爲他怕嚐試新的東西。」

「你完全答對了。」

⇨ Your plan hits the nail on the head.
你的計劃很好。

all ears
洗耳恭聽

⇨ What do you want to tell me？ I'm all ears.
你想告訴我什麼，我洗耳恭聽。

sweaty hands
毛手毛脚

⇨ Keep your sweaty hands off me, or you'll be sorry.
少毛手毛脚的，否則你會後悔。

lay fingers on
碰

⇨ Don't lay your fingers on me.
別碰我。

the long arm of the law
法網恢恢，疏而不漏

⇨ He finally got caught, 500 miles from home. He could not escape the long arm of the law.
他終於在離家五百哩的地方被捕了。眞是法網恢恢，疏而不漏。

long face
臭臉

⇨ John has a long face. He must have fought with his wife again. When you talk to him, be careful！
約翰今天擺了張臭臉，他一定又跟他太太吵了。你跟他講話時，小心一點！

on the tip of (*one's*)
tongue
話在舌尖

⇨ I can't think of his name. It's right on the tip of my tongue but I can't quite remember it.
我記不起他的名字。他的名字就在我嘴邊，但我一時想不起來。

on your feet 站起來
（多用於軍中的命令語）

⇨ On your feet and get moving.
站起來，走！

over my dead body
休想（除非我死了）

⇨ " Can I borrow your car？"
" Over my dead body."
「我能借你的車嗎？」
「休想。」

put my finger on
明白指出

⇨ There's something different about him but I just can't put my finger on it. 他有點不太一樣,但我又說不出來。

thumbs down
被拒絕；被否決

⇨ The decision on your proposal was thumbs down.
你的提議被否決了。

　＊ *thumbs up* 則是通過了。

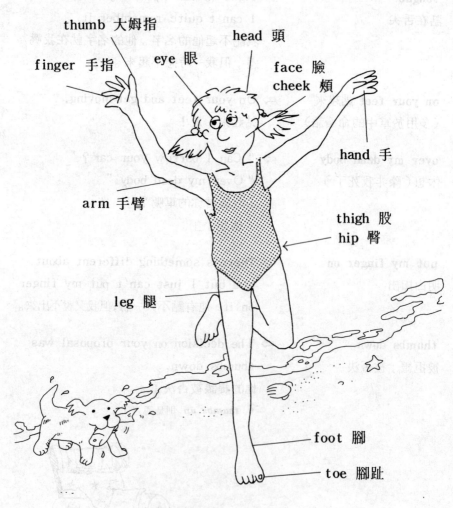

thumb 大姆指

head 頭

finger 手指

eye 眼

face 臉
cheek 頰

hand 手

arm 手臂

thigh 股
hip 臀

leg 腿

foot 腳

toe 腳趾

食物的聯想
INSPIRATION FROM FOOD

apples and oranges 兩
碼子事;不可混爲一談

⇨ You can't add apples and oranges.
兩件事不相關連，不可混爲一談。

as easy as cake
易如反掌；很容易

⇨ Breaking a brick with one hand is
as easy as cake for him. He's a
black-belt in Karate.
單手擊破一塊磚，對他而言易如反掌。因
爲他是空手道黑帶。

break the ice
誤會冰釋;打破僵局

⇨ Why don't you break the ice with
Linda? She didn't mean to hurt you.
你爲什麼不化解你跟琳達之間的誤會呢?
他不是存心要傷害你的。

⇨ Let's break the ice at this party and introduce ourselves to those girls over there.

讓我們打破舞會的僵局，過去跟那些女孩來個自我介紹。

cool as a cucumber
極其冷靜；不驚慌失措

⇨ After they heard the company was going to lay off 50 employees, everybody was in a panic. Jon, however, was cool as a cucumber.

在他們聽到公司將解僱 50 名人員之後，大家都十分驚慌，但是 Jon 却極其冷靜。

* cucumber〔ˈkjukʌmbɚ〕*n*. 胡瓜（俗稱黃瓜）

go bananas 發瘋

⇨ I'll go bananas if I have to do it again. 假如我得重頭再做一遍，我會發瘋。

⇨ If I stay with her for one more minute, I'll go bananas.

假如要我跟她再多待一分鐘，我會發瘋。

small potato
無足輕重的人

⇨ He's just a small potato.
他只是個無足輕重的人。

動物的聯想
INSPIRATION FROM ANIMALS

cast (*or throw*)
pearls before swine
對牛彈琴

⇨ She read us Byron's poems, but it was casting pearls to swine.
她對著我們朗誦拜倫的詩，那眞是對牛彈琴。

cat house 妓女戶

⇨ I went in there thinking it was a hotel. It turned out to be a cat house. 我走進去以爲那是一家旅社。結果却是一間妓女戶。

big frog in a small pond 山中無老虎，猴子稱霸王

⇨ He thinks he's a big shot at his company but he's really just a big frog in a small pond.
他以爲在他公司裏，他有多了不起，但只不過是山中無老虎，猴子稱霸王罷了。

chicken out 臨陣脫逃；
因膽怯而退出

⇨ I'm afraid he'll chicken out.
我怕他會臨陣脫逃。

* chicken〔'tʃɪkən〕*v.*〔俚〕臨陣脫逃

crocodile tears
貓哭耗子，假慈悲

⇨ "Jim, I'm sorry about you and Jane."
"Don't shed your crocodile tears
for me."
「吉米，我為你跟珍的事感到遺憾。」
「別貓哭耗子，假慈悲了。」

**curiosity killed the
cat** 好奇易招禍

⇨ Don't feel too bad about not knowing
what happened to her, you know,
curiosity killed the cat.
別為了不知道她的遭遇而感到太難過，你
知道，好奇會招來禍害的。

doggy（*or doggie*）
bag 裝剩餘飯菜用的
袋子

⇨ "Excuse me, could we have a doggy
bag to take this home？"
"Sure."
「對不起，能不能給我們一個袋子把這些
東西帶回家？」
「當然（可以）。」

monkey around 搗蛋

⇨ Don't monkey around here. I'm busy.
別在這兒搗蛋，我正在忙。

fat hog 肥豬

⇨ What are you eating again, fat hog？
你又在吃什麼了，肥豬？

gooney bird 笨鳥，笨蛋！

⇨ Who's that gooney bird？那個笨蛋是誰？

**hunt the same old
coon** 老幹某一行

⇨ I don't want to spend all my life
 hunting the same old coon.
 我可不想一輩子幹同樣的工作。

 ＊ coon〔kun〕*n.* 浣熊；樹狸

for the birds
沒意思

⇨ This book is for the birds.
 這本書眞沒意思。

night owl（ = *night
hawk*）夜貓子

⇨ I'm a night owl.
 我是個夜貓子。

old goat 老傢伙（不
客氣的說法）

⇨ Here comes the old goat. Be careful,
 he is very grouchy.
 那個老頭子又來了。小心點，他很暴躁。

 ＊ grouchy〔'grautʃɪ〕*adj.* 慍怒的；不悅的

英文片語趣味記憶法

編　　　著 / 武 藍 蕙

發 行 所 / 學習出版有限公司　　☎ (02) 2704-5525

郵 撥 帳 號 / 0512727-2 學習出版社帳戶

登 記 證 / 局版台業 2179 號

印 刷 所 / 裕強彩色印刷有限公司

台 北 門 市 / 台北市許昌街 10 號 2 F　☎ (02) 2331-4060・2331-9209

台灣總經銷 / 紅螞蟻圖書有限公司　☎ (02) 2795-3656

美國總經銷 / Evergreen Book Store　☎ (818) 2813622

本公司網址　www.learnbook.com.tw

電 子 郵 件　learnbook@learnbook.com.tw

書＋MP3 一片售價：新台幣一百八十元正

2009 年 11 月 1 日二版一刷

ISBN 9578-519-175-7